My So-Called Bollywood Life

MY SO-CALLED BOLLYWOOD LIFE

NISHA SHARMA

CROWN · NEW YORK

Text copyright © 2018 by Nisha Sharma
Jacket art copyright © 2018 by Aaron Sacco

All rights reserved. Published in the United States by Crown Books for Young Readers, an imprint of Random House Children's Books, a division of Penguin Random House LLC, New York.

Crown and the colophon are registered trademarks of Penguin Random House LLC.

Visit us on the Web! GetUnderlined.com

Educators and librarians, for a variety of teaching tools, visit us at RHTeachersLibrarians.com

Library of Congress Cataloging-in-Publication Data is available upon request.
ISBN 978-0-553-52325-6 (trade) — ISBN 978-0-553-52326-3 (lib. bdg.) — ISBN 978-0-553-52327-0 (ebook)

Printed in the United States of America
10 9 8 7 6 5 4 3 2 1
First Edition

Random House Children's Books supports the First Amendment and celebrates the right to read.

This book is dedicated to my mother, Neeta Sharma.
Thank you for buying me my first copy of *Pride and Prejudice*,
showing me that laughter is the best kind of medicine, and
teaching me that kitchen dancing is the only dancing I need.
This is what I've been working on instead of getting married and
giving you grandchildren. I think you'll like it.

Three years ago . . .

MY SO-CALLED BOLLYWOOD LIFE: A BLOG ABOUT THE HINDI LANGUAGE FILM INDUSTRY

Hello, blogging world! I'm starting high school this fall, where I'll be studying film, and I wanted to document the Bollywood movies that I'll be watching over the next four years. I'll be reviewing both old and new movies, but I'll focus on the New Bollywood era, which is the late '80s through the early 2000s. I love that period in Bollywood cinema.

Anyway.

Each blog entry will be a separate movie review, and because my best friend, Bridget, says she has a hard time keeping track of all the movies I talk about, I'll be translating the titles into English. I know, I know, they shouldn't be translated, but I doubt Bridget will pick up the language until an app offers it for free. (Hey, Bridget . . . if I can learn three languages, you can pick up freaking Hindi, dude.)

Reviews are totally my opinion, yada yada yada.

I can't WAIT to share my love of drama with all you guys. I don't have any drama in my own life, so this is the perfect way to get my fix.

1

From Winnie Mehta's Bollywood Review Blog:

QUEEN

★★★★☆

Kangana Ranaut's blockbuster included all the elements needed to create a money-making masterpiece: a strong woman, a stupid man, and tons of girl power.

According to Google, a grave was supposed to be six feet deep, but Winnie Mehta didn't want to put that much effort into digging. Besides, it wasn't as if she was dumping an actual body or anything.

She stopped and surveyed the burial site she'd chosen in the woods behind her house. After dragging three boxes and a shovel up the hiking path, Winnie had already built up a layer of sweat, but she had a lot to do before she could go home.

As she marked the hole, her phone began vibrating in her pocket. She sent the call to voice mail when she saw her best friend's face flash across the screen. That was Bridget's seventh call in the last hour. Winnie wanted—no, *needed*—

this moment, in which she stuck it to her stupid destiny, the wasted years she believed in true love, and, most importantly, to Raj, her cheating ex who'd hooked up with someone else while she was away at film camp. There was nothing Bridget could say that would change her mind.

It had been two months since Winnie had told Raj they needed a "break," which wasn't the same thing as a "breakup." And even if they had broken up, a relationship blossoming from a childhood romance that became official when they were fourteen deserved more than three weeks of mourning before one party moved on to someone else. Even celebrities waited longer than that.

The thought caused her hands to tighten on her shovel. She rolled her shoulders, and with a warrior's grunt, she started digging.

Stupid love story, stupid prophecy, stupid everything, she thought as she scooped up heaps of thick black soil. Since she was a kid, her family's astrologer had predicted that Winnie's soul mate would meet three unique criteria: his name would start with an *R*, he'd give her a silver bracelet as a sign of his love, and he'd cross paths with Winnie before her eighteenth birthday.

Identifying Raj as the man of her dreams wasn't too far-fetched, since they went to the same school and had grown up in the same community. Not to mention, he'd pulled out all the stops to get her to notice him when they were freshmen. For Winnie, accepting her destiny as truth and believing that her high school boyfriend was her soul mate for life was as easy as rattling off the top ten grossing Bollywood films per decade.

But then Raj changed. A lot. Three years later he wasn't her hipster in shining armor anymore. He'd traded in his collection of graphic T-shirts for polos and his love of movie nights for the tennis team and STEM club.

She felt her chest constrict and her heart pound from the exercise and from remembering that moment when Raj had told her he wanted to go to school in Boston instead of New York. He'd followed that truth bomb by asking her to give up her dreams and move to Boston, too.

"Winnie! Winnie, are you out here?" Bridget's voice echoed through the rustling trees and the sound of chirping birds. "I saw the drag marks from your car and across your backyard."

"Shit," she muttered. She started digging a little faster, tossing dirt in every direction.

"Okay, this is nuts," Bridget yelled. "Where the hell are you?"

Winnie tried to block the sounds of branches snapping as she continued to create her movie grave. Out of the corner of her eye, she saw Bridget step into the clearing. Her blond hair was tied in a high ponytail, and her shorts and tank were streaked with dirt, as if she'd wrestled her way through the rain forest instead of a small wooded area in Princeton, New Jersey.

"Oh. My. God," Bridget said as she pointed to the boxes. "Are those Raj's movies? You can't be serious! I get that I should've told you before you got back from camp this morning. It's just that I wanted to talk to you about this whole thing in person. I know it's a huge betrayal—"

"That's one way to put it."

"And you're probably pissed—"

Winnie froze. "'Probably pissed'? Are you freakin' kidding me?" She tossed the shovel to the ground and faced her friend. "No, I'd probably be pissed if I got a B in film class this year. I'd probably be pissed if I gained ten pounds and couldn't fit into my prom dress. I'm *murderous* right now because my boyfriend broke up with me online while basically announcing that he cheated! Did you know that he even wrote a Facebook post? My parents and their friends are the only ones who check Facebook. It's humiliating when your mother tells you that she saw the news on her feed. There are more people throwing me a pity party than extras in the movie *Gandhi*."

Bridget put up her hands in surrender. "I totally didn't know he was going to do that, but to be fair, I did warn you that he was hanging out with Jenny Dickens."

The second she heard Jenny's name, Winnie hocked a loogie. Well, she tried, but she ended up choking and coughing on her own spit.

"What the hell was that?"

"I can't hear that man-stealing backstabber's name without spitting," Winnie said, pressing a fist to her chest. "It's a demonstration of how I feel about her."

Bridget snorted. "What movie did you see that one in?"

"It's not funny, Bridget! Damn it, it wasn't supposed to end like this." To her horror, tears started to fill her eyes.

"Oh crap," Bridget said, and scrambled forward. The second Winnie felt her friend's tight hug, a sob broke through her throat. Then another followed, and another, until she couldn't stop.

Bridget held her while she cried for the first time since she'd realized her love story was finally over. Memories circled in her mind like vultures. First kiss, themed dates, Bollywood marathons, film festivals, passionate arguments over movies. She knew that Raj believed in her prophecy because of all the effort that he'd invested in their relationship. Just when she'd started thinking that maybe Raj really was the answer to her family astrologer's prediction for a happily-ever-after, he changed. Now their relationship was a short caption in a yearbook. They were the cliché high school romance.

What a joke.

Winnie pulled away and wiped her face with the hem of her tank top. "I should've known that Pandit Ohmi was wrong," she said, sniffling. "What was I thinking? I was brainwashed. This proves it."

"Just because Raj isn't *the* soul mate doesn't mean that

your soul mate doesn't exist," Bridget said. "There are tons of guys out there whose names start with *R* and who'll give you a silver bracelet."

Winnie stepped to the edge of the hole and sat down in the fresh dirt. "You and I both know I'm not going to find someone else who fits Pandit Ohmi's prediction—not before I'm eighteen, at any rate. The way my parents have crammed it down my throat all these years, it's as if Raj's name is practically written in with the prophecy."

"Obviously that's not true," Bridget said as she sat down next to Winnie.

Whoever coined the phrase "truth hurts" was probably a smug jackass, Winnie thought.

"If he was really the guy for me," she said between sniffles, "then we should've been able to work past this, right? Like a growing pain. We were great for the first two years, but junior year was so hard, and I needed some space, some time to breathe and think about what he wanted from me. So, like an idiot, I spent the summer thinking, and he spent the summer forgetting. It sucks, but we're too different now to work things out. Cheating puts the last nail in our relationship's coffin . . . which is why I'm digging a grave." She motioned to the shallow hole at her feet. "To bury my coffin."

"If you know you two aren't going to work anymore, then why are you so mad at him for hooking up with Jenny? You should be happy that it's over."

"Because I stayed faithful," Winnie said as she dug her sneakered toe into the dirt. Her heart ached a little as she said the words. "He moved on to someone else without a second thought. Plus, he wasn't honest. We were friends before we dated, Bridge. I thought maybe we could go back to that if things didn't work out. But now? I've lost a friend, too."

"Well, screw him," Bridget said. "He sucks."

Winnie wiped her nose. "I can confidently say that soul mates are for the movies."

"I don't know why you trusted the whole prophecy thing," she said. "We're talking about a prediction a psychic made."

"He's not a psychic. He's an astrologer. A priest. A pandit."

Bridget stood up and walked over to one of the boxes piled high with DVDs. She kicked the side of it, and the contents rattled. "Sounds like a psychic to the blonde here."

"He's pretty accurate, Bridge. He reads charts based on star alignments that were in the sky when someone was born. It's a religious thing. Or is it a cultural thing? Either way, it's something important."

"That you don't believe in anymore," she said.

Winnie winced. "Yeah, I guess not." But a part of her wished that it was still true. Maybe a part of her still wanted it to happen. But to what end? She was going to be disappointed if she kept hoping that Raj would change back into the guy she remembered.

"Forget about the prophecy and how much it sucks that

you believed it," Bridget said. "Eat ice cream and pizza, and watch your favorite movies. We'll get frappes and binge on some new show. You know, the normal coping things."

Winnie stood and brushed the dirt off the seat of her pants. "I've never been dumped before. This blows."

"Welcome to my life."

Winnie should've never ignored Bridget's calls. She needed her bestie more than she needed revenge. "Thanks for being my best freaking friend for life, Bridge."

"You know I'm here. Ugh, I hate that you don't get all red and blotchy-eyed. I can't even tell that you've been crying."

Winnie laughed for the first time all day and squeezed Bridget in a death grip. "I hate that your hair doesn't get frizzy in the humidity."

"Touché," Bridget said. "Come on, let's get these back to Raj."

"Um, no." Winnie pulled away and circled the hole she'd started. "I dug my grave. I now have to live with it. Besides, it's not really his stuff. It's just whatever I bought for him during the time we were together. I never realized how many movies I gave him until I was taking them out of his house."

Bridget picked up one of the external hard drives. She waved it in front of Winnie's face. "You did not buy him this."

"No, that's actually mine that he was borrowing. It's been tainted by his cheating hands, so I'm burying it, too."

"Wow, you actually mean that. Okay, I know where you're coming from, but you're going to end up screwing yourself over. Can't you put this in a post online and delete it later? You have to face facts. Everyone at school loves Raj, even if he's the one who broke up with you."

"I don't get how I could possibly be the bad guy," Winnie grumbled.

"Duh. He's the film nerd who became captain of the tennis team and won a mathlete competition on the same day he worked the film festival. He's the golden boy who's taking the STEM track and the arts track. He's one of the few double-track students in our history that everyone loves."

"I don't care. I have to do this," Winnie said. "It's like I'm burying the hatchet or something. I don't even know what a hatchet is, but it applies here."

"You gave this stuff to him. It belongs to Raj now. If people found out you broke into his house and took his things after you were the one who asked for space, it makes you look like the guilty person, not him."

"If you don't like what I'm doing, then you can leave. Or you can stay and help me with all of this." She motioned to the mounds of dirt she'd already displaced. "But I'm warning you, I may bury my copy of *Pride and Prejudice* that I loaned to Raj last summer."

Bridget froze. "Which version?"

"BBC."

She went ashen. "You'd bury Colin? You've lost your mind! This is blackmail."

"And it works. Listen, I'm not exactly enjoying this new

criminal lifestyle. I know taking Raj's movies wasn't my best moment, but doing this matters to me. I'll have to deal with the consequences later, but right now, I'm going to dig."

Bridget's face morphed from anger to panic and finally resolve. Winnie felt a shining silver lining appear on her rain cloud.

"Fine. You win." She waited a beat before pointing to Winnie's bare wrist. "On one condition. Did you get rid of the bracelet?"

Winnie ignored the feel of the jewelry in her pocket. She knew it wasn't right to keep it, but she needed some more time before she buried that final piece of her past. If she told Bridget her reasoning, her best friend wouldn't understand. So she kept both the truth and the bracelet tucked away. "Yeah, it's gone already."

"Good. I didn't say it when he gave it to you, but I never really liked that thing. Totally not your style." Bridget sighed before she gestured. "But that still leaves this stuff to deal with. How did you get it all?"

"Raj gave me the code to the garage a year ago or so. His family was at temple, so the timing was great. Their schedule is always the same on weekends."

"What about Raj?"

Winnie pulled up his profile on her phone. Bridget leaned in, eyes squinting.

"'With my girl to get ice cream. Jenny is as sweet as her favorite kind: strawberries and cream.' Ugh, barf!"

"I know, right? That has to be the most disgusting flavor ever."

"I'm surprised she could taste anything with all that lipstick getting in the way," Bridget said. "Who would've thought Raj would date someone like Jenny after you? Especially since he looks like the poster boy for an Ivy League these days. All old money."

Winnie's stomach twisted when she read the post again. "Who cares? His sappy update was definitely useful. I was in and out of the house in five minutes."

"Winnie!"

"What? I told you. Not one of my best moments."

"Fine. If I'm blackmailed into doing this, let's get it over with. Best friends help each other bury the body, right?"

"Right," Winnie said with a grin. Some of the pain she was feeling dimmed as Bridget stepped up next to her and grabbed the shovel.

They took turns digging until the hole was at least three feet deep. Then, with some huffing and puffing, they dragged the boxes filled with DVDs, Blu-rays, and external hard drives to the edge of their amateur grave.

Winnie looked down at the contents of her loot. On top of the pile sat the 2007 ten-year-anniversary collector's edition of the movie *Dil To Pagal Hai,* the infamous film that had an eerie similarity to her horoscope. Winnie had purchased a copy for Raj when they first started dating.

She ran her finger over the faces on the cover. Shah Rukh

Khan, the hero of the movie, sporting a massive mullet, had his arms around the heroine's waist as she curved against him in her shiny black unitard with matching sweatbands. As far as Bollywood flicks went, it was a classic late-nineties love triangle.

The part of the story Winnie had always loved was when the hero recognized the heroine as his mystery woman from the sound of her bracelet jingling as she walked away. The bracelet in the movie was nothing like the one Raj had given her, though. Maybe that should've been a clue that Raj was wrong for her.

Winnie threw the DVD into the hole and flinched when she saw the bright neon, jewel-toned cover lying against the stark brown dirt. Seeing one of their favorite movies like that was harder than she expected.

"Come on," Bridget said softly. "Keep going. It'll get easier."

Winnie resumed tossing the contents, silently saying goodbye to the memory associated with each movie. No more dates, no more dances, no more future together at the same college in New York. She'd just have to do it all alone.

When they finished filling the hole, Bridget wrapped an arm around Winnie's shoulders and squeezed. "We're good, right?"

"I really don't know," Winnie said after a moment. The whole experience had been a bit cathartic, but like any good movie, there was still a lot of plot left to work through. "Now that I'm done, I should probably start thinking about Monday. I don't know how we're going to be co-presidents of the film club if Raj makes things awkward."

Bridget rubbed her arm. "Don't worry about that now. Enjoy your moment of revenge. It'll all be a bad dream when you're studying at NYU. You'll be rocking in film school while Raj will still be mourning the loss of the stuff that you bought him. No pictures because you don't want evidence, but definitely commit this to memory."

"To memory, huh?"

"Yup, this is the end of something, right?" She motioned to the hole, to the empty boxes and the shovel. "The end of something is like a shooting star. Gone in a second."

"Okay," Winnie said with a whoosh of air. "Okay, I can remember this." Winnie cupped her hands in front of her eyes in the shape of a heart. She saw only images of famous actors and actresses, movie titles, and taglines in a blur of color. She jerked her hands apart, tearing the makeshift heart in two. She was able to see the full picture now: the displaced dirt and the poor condition of the movies. Things were always clearer in panorama.

"Got any last words?" Bridget said.

"Yeah. Yeah, I do. *Fin.* After all, this is the end, right? So . . . *Fin.*"

Winnie picked up the shovel.

2

WHAT'S YOUR RAASHEE? / WHAT'S YOUR HOROSCOPE?
★★☆☆☆

It's a new era in Bollywood. Astrologer priests no longer dress in lungis and work in isolation. It's the 21st century, and sometimes astrologers can look like you and me.

Winnie cracked open her bedroom door and listened for the sounds of her parents settling down in the living room. When she heard the opening music of *Indian Idol* starting, she knew that they'd be preoccupied long enough for her to have a private conversation.

She settled on the center of her bed with her laptop and clicked on the v-chat icon so she could connect with the username she'd gotten from her grandmother. Even though it was early morning in India, twelve hours ahead, Winnie hoped the famous Pandit Ohmi would take her video conference call. She'd never spoken to the priest directly, but she figured that since her mother talked to him every two months or so, he wouldn't mind talking to her, too.

She straightened her shoulders and yanked up the neckline of her shirt to cover any exposed cleavage. While she waited for the feed to load, she wondered if he'd be offended because she wasn't dressed like she was going to temple. Her head wasn't covered, and her arms and legs were bare. Winnie's parents hadn't prepared her for this sort of thing, and she'd never been around to watch her mother talk to Pandit Ohmi. She should've checked online. After her conversation, she'd blog about it so other people could know what to wear when telling off an Indian priest/astrologer.

The slender face of a grandfather-like man filled her screen. A long line of red powder streaked up the middle of his forehead from the center of his bushy eyebrows to what would've been a hairline if he wasn't bald. He peered at her through silver metal-framed glasses that looked like they'd seen better days. The hair sticking out of his nostrils flared.

"Is that the young Vaneeta Mehta?" he asked in Hindi. "Yes, it must be you. But yet it is not Vaneeta. Winnie is what you go by. Your grandmother has called you that since you were in diapers, nah?"

"Whoa." Maybe she looked more like her grandmother and mother than she thought. They did share the same wide-set eyes and thickly arched eyebrows that were whipped into shape thanks to frequent trips to a threading salon.

When his forehead wrinkled, Winnie cleared her throat and responded in the same language. "Yes, I am Winnie. I hope I am not interrupted, but I don't know if there is a right time I could talk in you. I have request."

Okay, that sounded weird even to her. She knew she was screwing up her verb tenses again—and maybe some other stuff, too—but hopefully he got the gist.

Pandit Ohmi steepled his fingers and nodded. "You can speak in English. I understand that as well as your Hindi."

Thank the gods, Winnie thought. She could understand the languages that her parents spoke, but actually speaking Hindi and Punjabi was a little trickier.

"Okay, awesome. Uh, thanks for answering my call. I wanted to talk to you about the janampatri reading you did for my mother when I was a baby."

"Oh ho," he said, clucking his tongue after a pause. "So sorry about the death of your young romance."

"My mother already got to you? Great," she said, and dropped her head into her hands.

"She's concerned for you. And no, I haven't spoken to her yet. Your face has a story written onto it that I read very quickly."

Winnie heard a few clicks as he leaned in closer to examine something on his computer monitor. "Ah, here is your family file. Mm-hmm, it looks here like your love story has changed in the last year, but your overall celestial alignment hasn't altered. Your star chart provides the same prophecy it did seventeen and a half years ago, except now you have already met your love."

"No way. How can Raj still be the one when it doesn't . . . I don't know, *feel* like he's the right guy anymore?"

"Who says it's still Raj?"

Winnie sighed. "But, Panditji, it can't be anyone else. Trust me, I know. Raj is the only one who fits your profile, and he has changed in the past year."

"We all change. That is what growing up is all about."

"Not like this. Okay, let me set the scene. His dad is an engineer who registered this patent and made a ton of money. Raj now wants to be an engineer, too. It's like he never wanted to be a film critic like me, even though we've been talking about that for our entire lives, and . . ." She trailed off when she realized what she was saying. Pandit Ohmi was the root of her problem, and if she gave him too many details about her life, then he could use them against her by creating another dumb prophecy for her mother to harass her about. Shifting on the bed, she pushed her long hair over her shoulders. "Never mind. Basically, Raj isn't for me."

He shook his finger at the screen, and the gold ring on it glinted. "I think I understand. Your and your parents' star charts are the most beautiful I've ever read. You're afraid that if it comes true, you'll be disappointed because it's a choice you didn't make. But wouldn't you be equally disappointed if it didn't come true? Finding a jeevansathi is a gift that many people aren't fortunate enough to receive."

Jeevansathi. Life partner. Soul mate. She looked over at her dresser and saw the promise of Raj's silver bracelet. Keep cool, she thought. Keep it cool. He might be super accurate, but he was wrong about this. He was wrong about her.

"Listen, I know you did this huge awesome prediction for my folks before they first got married, but I think you're wrong this time around. I think that you watched *Dil To Pagal Hai* one too many times and maybe superimposed that Bollywood plotline onto me and thought, hey, this is totally plausible. I appreciate the peace of mind you give to my mother, but please don't talk to her about my soul mate story deal anymore. I'd like for my folks to eventually get over it, you know?"

"Vaneeta, you want to study the arts?"

Shouldn't he have known that already? And how was that relevant at all? She bit back her snark and answered him anyway. "Sort of, yeah. Movies. I want to study them."

"Your father wanted to be in the arts. He didn't do it."

She softened a little bit at the thought of her dad and the way he lit up like a Diwali candle whenever he spoke about movies. "He wanted to do something in the film business, but it didn't work out. Everyone told him that he had to go with his prophecy that *you* predicted based on his star chart."

"Don't you think marrying your mother is a choice he willingly made?"

Winnie's father never said he regretted getting married, but sometimes, when they watched movies together, his face would glow, and then he'd get so sad that even she could feel it, while sitting inches from him on the couch. Now that Raj was no longer in the picture, Winnie could see that if she hadn't loved film more than she loved her boyfriend, she could've ended up in the same situation. The thought made her sweat.

"He loved my mom."

Pandit Ohmi grinned and waved a hand at the camera as if shooing her off. "Yes, and he still loves movies. You'll make him very proud with whatever you do, but I hope it's because you get a happily-ever-after by choice or by chance. Your astrological chart shows that there are a lot of pitfalls in the next few months that can prevent that from happening, but I am confident that you will find your way."

"Wait, pitfalls?" Her mind raced with everything that could go wrong. Everyone at school could turn on her for crushing Raj's heart, even though he was the one who cheated. The film festival could be a horror show. If they made enough money at the fund-raiser dance to even have a festival.

Or worse. She might not get into NYU's Tisch School of the Arts. She'd be stuck going to a local school where she had to be a theater major and commute from home instead of dorming.

Nope. Not happening.

"Don't tell me—I'm not interested." Winnie scrubbed her hands over her face. She couldn't get herself wrapped up in Pandit Ohmi's storytelling. She needed to do her thing and ignore the Hindu stuff.

Pandit Ohmi laughed. "Sometimes ignorance truly is bliss."

"Thanks for the tip, but all I'm asking is that you stop telling Mom about the prophecy."

"Take care of yourself, Vaneeta Mehta. Say hello to your parents for me."

Winnie closed the v-chat window. She shouldn't care.

Before she could get up and get ready for bed, her phone vibrated.

"Hi, Nani," she said when she answered.

Her grandmother's nose filled the screen. "Hi, beta," she shouted. The Hindi word for "child."

"Nani, first, you're calling from Long Island, not India. I can hear you just fine. Second, the phone is too close."

Nani pulled the phone away. Her shining face was creased with very few wrinkles for a woman in her late sixties. Her hair was streaked with orange from the henna she used to dye the few gray strands, and she wore what looked like a velvet tracksuit.

"Is this better?" she said, still yelling.

Winnie grinned. "It's fine. I miss you."

Nani lifted a copper tumbler to her lips before responding. "I miss my baby, too. Why don't you call me more?"

"I talked to you last week."

"Too long ago," she said in Hindi. She switched to Punjabi and added, "What is happening in your life? How is this boy, Raj?"

Switching between languages was common practice for

Winnie, but she almost always spoke English with her parents. Probably because they tended to make fun of her accent. But with her grandmother she could say whatever she wanted in whatever language she wanted to use while she butchered her grammar. Nani was her safe space. Always.

"Raj and I are not one with each other," Winnie said in broken Punjabi. She then explained what had happened and how she'd asked Pandit Ohmi to stop with the prophecy talk. Nani listened, humming occasionally in agreement, until Winnie finished.

"I know you don't like to hear it, but maybe Pandit Ohmi is right. Your destiny hasn't changed, and Raj will stop being a bewakoof idiot boy."

Winnie held the phone above her head. "I don't know, Nani. I'm thinking I should focus on this film festival that my club is hosting. I'm still mad about the way Raj broke things off, but it's time to look toward my future. I'm done with romance."

Nani snorted. "You're Indian! We live for romance. And when there is romance, there is passion. Where is your sense of passion right now, beta? Without both romance and passion, you'll be as boring as Raj's mother."

"Nani!"

"What? I've met her. She's boring."

Winnie laughed. "I may love rom-coms, Nani, and I'm definitely passionate about film school, but I'm also aware that star charts aren't the answer to everything."

"And yet those star charts led me to your nana and connected your parents."

"Luck. There is also such a thing as luck."

Nani narrowed her eyes. "You sound like you are trying to convince yourself of something you don't believe. I think I need to come there and smack some sense into you."

"You should! It's been so long since you've visited. What are you drinking, by the way? Mango lassi?"

Nani looked down at her cup and then up at the screen. "Oh, look at the time. I better go. Bye, beta. Love you!"

Winnie laughed. "Love you, too, Nani." She hung up and flopped on the bed. Even her grandmother, her staunchest supporter, couldn't see things her way. Or maybe she was having a hard time convincing other people that her star chart was wrong because she couldn't really convince herself.

In her dream, Winnie ran through the fields in a pink gown with lace sleeves. Her hair was crowned with fake white flowers and a long lace veil. She could smell the sunshine and feel the spongy grass under her feet as she traveled up the gentle slope of a hill.

Winnie knew that someone was waiting for her at the top. Anticipation pumped through her, which only spurred her to quicken her pace. The train of her dress trailed behind her, and the jewel-encrusted sandals were fashionable yet functional enough for heroine field running.

In the distance, mountains rolled into a blue sea. She scanned the horizon, and that's when she saw him. He wore black pants, a black billowing shirt, a cape, a wide-brimmed hat, and a Zorro mask.

He spun, arms outstretched.

"Shah Rukh Khan from Baazigar?" Winnie said, jaw dropping. "Is that you?" Her voice traveled over the green fields and across the cliffs.

King Khan, the superstar of Bollywood superstars, tore off the mask and lifted an eyebrow in his signature look.

"Why, yes, señorita, it is I."

Winnie shoved her billowing hair from her face. "You quoted one of your movies! Not Baazigar, but still one of your movies. This is the best dream of my life."

Shah Rukh Khan swaggered toward her. "I've come to deliver a message to you to relieve your doubt."

"My doubt of what?"

"Of destiny," he said. "Because those who fight destiny, who fight what's written in the stars, always end up having the hardest struggle."

When she reached his side, he gripped her hand and twirled her in a circle. Her veil floated around her shoulders.

"Well, I don't like my destiny anymore," she said when

she stopped spinning. "I can change it if I want to. It's the twenty-first century, Shah Rukh. Not everything is about love anymore. Look at the film industry."

"You're right," he said, and lowered her into a dip. "So are you ready to struggle?"

She was just imagining things because of what Pandit Ohmi said to her that night. None of this was real. But since she was dancing with Shah Rukh Khan and she had nothing to lose, she asked, "You got any advice?"

He pulled her up and in Hindi said, "In life, if you want to become, achieve, or win something, then listen to your heart. If your heart doesn't say something to you, then close your eyes and take the names of your mother and father like a mantra. Then watch. You'll achieve everything, and whatever was difficult will become easy. Victory will be yours."

"Now you're quoting Kabhi Khushi Kabhie Gham! *That's the most noncommittal advice ever, Shah Rukh," she said. Since he was in her dream, she figured she had the right to call him by his first names. "The title of the movie is noncommittal, too. 'Sometimes Happiness, Sometimes Sadness'? Come on."*

"It works," he said with another laugh.

"And I'm assuming, since you're a parent and all, that you're telling me to listen to my folks. But this is my dream, and I do what I want!"

"You always have, dost."

Friend.

He let go of her hand and started backing away toward the cliff, and fog began rolling in. Winnie waved at the fog, trying to keep him in sight, but Shah Rukh Khan's image faded as he slipped into the cloud. The only lingering part of him was his voice.

"Remember, Winnie Mehta, fighting fate never works. I've made a career out of proving just how powerful destiny can be."

Winnie jerked up in bed. She could feel the dampness at her hairline and on her neck.

"Holy baby Shah Rukh Khan," she whispered. What was she supposed to make of *that*?

She powered up her laptop, which was sitting on the pillow next to her, and rubbed her eyes, trying to clear her vision. After a few clicks, she squinted at the screen to make out the last few movies she'd streamed.

"Come on, where are you?" she said into the dark. She knew it had been years since she'd watched *Baazigar,* but she had to have seen *Kabhi Khushi Kabhie Gham* recently. When she couldn't find the movie in her active playlist, she checked her archives.

She hadn't watched it in ages, either.

So why had she dreamed about it?

There was only one way to find out. She clicked on the movie title and put in her earbuds. With a yawn, she settled in against her pillows, hoping that rewatching the film could help her make sense of what she'd just dreamed.

3

STUDENT OF THE YEAR
★★★★☆

High school hallways are always shot in the same way. Groups of people whispering and huddled in corners. Oddly enough, the only thing different from real life is the background music that follows the heroine around like a rain cloud.

The Princeton Academy for the Arts and Sciences was a selective institution that thrived on excellence in acting, dance, music, and film as well as STEM programs. At any given moment, someone could burst into song in the cafeteria, jeté down the hallway, or pull out an AP Physics textbook.

Winnie squeezed through a group of cute-bots wearing leotards and UGGs before she reached her locker. Since the first bell, she had forced herself to be polite, sometimes flippant, sometimes funny about the whole Raj thing. No one thought for a second how much her pride, or even her heart, was hurting. Now she needed a moment to chill, so she concentrated on the collage of her favorite Bollywood actors centered inside her locker door that she'd put together that morning. Her senior year class schedule was pasted above the collage, and a list of upcoming Bollywood and art-house movies were below, followed by her blog review calendar. At the bottom were key film-club event dates she'd scheduled at the end of her junior year with the faculty advisor, Ms. Jackson.

She ran her hand over a random sticky note that had the name of a local movie theater, a date, and the words *'80s movie night* along with *Say Anything* circled in red pen. Bridget's obsession with eighties movies rivaled her love for Jane Austen, and seeing something other than a Shah Rukh Khan blockbuster was always a great distraction.

Winnie was exhausted from her sleepless night, but the first meeting for film club was in half an hour, and because Raj had changed to STEM classes, Winnie still hadn't gotten a chance to talk to him. She'd sent him a text with film-club-related questions in second period, but he'd yet to respond.

She was working through potential scenarios on how the first meeting would go, tossing books in her bag, when someone tapped her on the shoulder. Winnie jumped and muffled a shriek.

"Whoa," Bridget said, pointing at her face. "Put that fake smile away. It's creepy."

"Bridge. You have no idea how happy I am to see you," she said, pressing a hand to her thudding heart. "People are *still* talking about my breakup! You'd think that something like this wouldn't be a big deal."

"Well, scandal, especially between film-club presidents, needs some discussion time."

Winnie rolled her eyes. "Even Rebecca Peterson stopped me today."

"Isn't she the one who always put out your Bunsen burner in Gen Chem because of her mouth breathing?"

"That's the one."

"Apparently, she tells people that it's helpful when she plays the sax. I bet her mouth blows up like a blowfish when she sucks in air and holds her breath, sort of like Miles Davis. Was it Miles Davis who played the sax? I should text my mom. She'll know."

"Focus, Bridge."

"Yeah, okay. What did she say?"

"She asked what was going on. I told her it was all true and that Jenny 'Dick-in' even tattooed Raj's name on her body in Sanskrit characters, the same way that Chase Evans tattooed Rebecca's name over his heart."

Bridget grinned and shoved Winnie's shoulder. "Poor Chase! Sax-y Rebecca is going to be all over him now."

"I felt bad, but honestly, what am I supposed to say? That I asked for a break first? I doubt people want to hear about my head trip. Like, I'm not sure if I'm mad about the way the breakup happened or about no longer having a boyfriend. I'm definitely hurting because I'm not going to have my soul mate prophecy like my parents, but was it stupid of me to believe in star charts in the first place? And Raj's fan club is going to tar and feather me if I admit that Raj isn't the same guy that I started dating years ago, and that I'm not sure I even like the person he is now. I feel none of that big block-buster, drama-style grief, either. It's all confusing. I'm in the middle of an ocean, like Tom Hanks's volleyball."

"Speaking of Raj, have you talked to him?"

"No!" Winnie said, slamming her locker door. They started walking toward the auditorium. "Can you believe it? I've known him since I was six freaking years old and I saw him every day for three of the past eleven years. Because of his new schedule, it's as if we don't even go to the same school. Do you think he's angry I took my stuff? He should at least say something to me about it, right? Or at least about the bracelet he bought me."

"I doubt he'll mention it. He always let you do the con-fronting. At least you don't have to worry about film club, since you and Ms. Jackson have already set the calendar. She'll have your back about the festival, too. All you have to do is think about how you're going to look when everyone sees you together onstage."

They were halfway to their destination when Winnie saw a familiar face. Henry Donald Richardson V, his shoulders hunched, his skinny arms held tight to his side, kicked his locker before opening it. Winnie noticed that his Tardis T-shirt had seen better days, and his black painted nails matched the exact shade of his black shoulder-length hair.

"Hi, Henry," Bridget called out. "Looking good."

He fumbled with his bag and dropped it. "Hi." He flushed when Bridget wiggled her fingers at him.

Winnie shot Bridget a questioning look before she asked Henry, "Heading to the meeting?"

"Nope. Raj can suck a mother ship. I'm leaving film club."

"What?" Winnie choked out. "Why? We need you and your techies!"

"Not according to Raj. Dude said he'd handle all the tech stuff himself along with his new mathlete freaks because I told him he was acting like a prick these days."

"No!" Winnie and Bridget said in unison.

"He's not one of us anymore. I refuse to put up with his crap any longer. You probably know how that feels more than anyone, Winnie. I gotta get home. It's good seeing you."

"Hey, if you ever want in, please call me! You and the AV tech-sperts are always welcome."

Henry walked backward, his arms spread wide. "You guys should get going. If the meeting is about to start, you don't want Raj to change the film club into one of the science clubs, too."

Winnie watched him leave. "Holy baby Shah Rukh Khan. This is really happening."

Bridget gripped Winnie's upper arms and shook. "Keep it together, Mehta. You were doing so well."

She pulled out of Bridget's grip. "You think shaking me hard enough to loosen my cavities is going to make me better?" Winnie muttered. She took in a deep yoga-like breath, and started down the hall again. She hadn't been this nervous even when she got the acceptance letter from NYU film camp.

"Don't think about it," Bridget said. "Just walk in, swinging your hips, with that smile on your face. You'll stun and scare them all."

"I guess. It's the only ammunition I have right now. At least Ms. Jackson knows how much work I put in last year, so hopefully if I start to babble, she'll cover."

They'd almost reached the double doors leading into the auditorium that had been Winnie's favorite place for years until the day she'd asked Raj for the space she needed to think. That was right after he told her he wasn't going to apply to NYU. He wanted to go to a fancy engineering school in Boston, and he expected her to go with him.

"You can do this. I know you can," Bridget said, taking Winnie's backpack from her. "You've always been a talker. Even if you're broken up, you'll be able to figure it out."

"Yeah? Okay. Okay, you're right. Bridge? I don't know what I'd do without you. I owe you," Winnie said.

Raj. The film festival. The stupid prophecy. Everyone watching. All of it was running through her head as she flung open the doors to the auditorium and put on her most brilliant smile for the show.

The members took up the first three rows, facing a lean Indian guy onstage. His hand froze midair.

That's right, she thought. Hello, Raj, I'm back.

She sauntered down the aisle, putting in an extra swing to her swagger. It was do-or-die time. "Am I late?" she said cheerfully. "Sorry about that. Thanks for waiting for me, guys."

Raj stood on the stage, under the spotlight, something he'd grown fond of over the last year. It had been a couple of months, but he looked like he had when she'd last seen him. Even from a distance she could see his gelled hair, tight jeans, and designer polo shirt.

If her life was a movie, a strain of horrible violin music would be playing in the background while images of past regrets whirled like a rotating screen around her head.

"Hey, Raj. Hey, everyone!" Her smile froze when she saw Mr. Reece sitting in the front row. She faltered midstride.

"Mr. Reece."

"Ms. Mehta." He stood up, adjusting his tweed jacket over his Captain America T-shirt and pushing at the bridge of his glasses. "Nice of you to finally show up."

"Uh, are you stepping in for Ms. Jackson? Is she sick?"

"In a manner of speaking," he said. "If you'd been on time, then you would've heard when I announced that Ms. Jackson is expecting, and can't commit to any extracurricular groups this year. That's why you get me. I know you're so excited to have one of us science geniuses as your faculty advisor, but as a former stunt double for Wil Wheaton, I do have film experience. Raj asked me this morning if I was interested."

Winnie's dread ballooned, but she managed to choke out,

"Ms. Jackson didn't say anything to me. Raj didn't check with . . . great. This is . . . great."

He raised an eyebrow. "Come now, Ms. Mehta. In the three years I've had you in my science classes, you've never shied from the truth."

This time she did smile. As teacher and student, they'd had a love-hate relationship. Most of the time, Winnie had tried to love him, while she was sure Mr. Reece hated her. "Did you get my present from camp?"

"I do enjoy a good three-D puzzle of the Death Star. But I don't know how many times I've had to tell you that my acting mentor was in *Star Trek,* not *Star Wars.*"

"It was a joke."

"Ha ha. As bribes go, you should've sent a fruit basket like everyone else."

"*Bribe* is such a dirty word, Mr. Reece," Winnie said. "After all those mandatory classes you and I have been through over the years. I like to think of it as incentive."

"It didn't work."

"I still got an A in physics last year."

"That's because I grade on merit, not on taste," he said. Some people in the audience started laughing.

She ascended the stage and scanned the familiar faces of other board members in their class, the pitying expressions of underclassmen, and the supportive smiles of a few people she was grateful she could count on. She turned to Raj.

"Hey," she said.

"Hey, Winnie." He tried to smile at her, too, and shoved his hands in his front jeans pockets. Winnie felt the tears burn in her throat. Oh shit, she thought.

A piercing whistle snapped her out of her spiraling thoughts. Dev Khanna lounged in the back row. His molasses brown eyes fixed on hers, and for one moment something clicked in her head, like a frame locking into place.

Dev and she had been sharing weird looks since the beginning of freshman year. They'd been on their way to becoming friends—she'd been sure of it—but then he'd stopped talking to her when she started dating Raj, probably since Dev was the only person who hated her now ex.

"Thanks for that, Dev!" she shouted. The sound of laughter had her striking a pose automatically, hoping that no one noticed that her hands were still shaking.

"Your ex looks way better now that you're not with her, Shah!" Dev called.

The auditorium boomed with laughter, and although Winnie's insides were twisted, she kept smiling. Raj, on the other hand, looked like he was about to commit murder.

"Okay, everyone. Settle down," Mr. Reece said. "We have an agenda to stick to."

"Why don't you start," Raj said. He reached into his pocket for his phone. "I was going to read your text anyway if you weren't going to . . . show or something. And sorry about Ms. Jackson. I should've known she'd forget to tell you in person. She sent us both an email early this morning."

"Oh. Well, I should've checked my email, I guess."

She smiled at the audience as brightly as she could. "It's a new year and we have the calendar of movie showings on the group site. All we have to do is make sure we have the projector and donation box set up at each event."

Winnie went through her talking points, fielding questions from Mr. Reece and making notes on her phone when she had an action item. Raj stood silently at her side, with his legs braced.

"Do you want to add anything?" she said when she finished.

He shook his head. "You've got this."

"Great. The last thing I wanted to talk about is our biggest event. The film festival!"

Cheers erupted in the auditorium. Winnie grinned. "I checked the submission portal, and it looks like students from all over the U.S. are already sending in their shorts. We'll have sign-ups on the group site for the committees. Now, we usually do things like a car wash, an international bake sale, or a screening, but we are going to try something different this year. The film club is hosting a school dance. It's in a couple months, so please plan on attending. We need the extra funds for our operating budget. I'll let you know when I do—"

"Wait," Mr. Reece said, standing up. "I thought one of you handled the film festival and the other oversaw the club activities."

"Well, the job has a lot of crossover, so Ms. Jackson assigns co-presidents to take care of both. That way everything is covered and all projects have a backup."

"But that's against the rules for student clubs," Mr. Reece said. "There can only be one president, and all major events have to be led by another member of the club."

Winnie looked at Raj. "But that's always how film club has worked. Since we were freshmen."

Mr. Reece shook his head. "I'm going to have to talk to Ms. Jackson about this, because it sounds like there is an imbalance of workload here. School rules are school rules."

Winnie felt a sinking sensation in her stomach again. Before Winnie could comment, she saw Bridget waving from the crowd. *Let it go,* she mouthed.

Winnie had to count to five before she responded. "Okay, then, next week we'll talk about the festival location at Princeton University."

"That's fine," Mr. Reece said. He looked at his wristwatch. "Since I have to leave for a prior obligation, we can call an end to the meeting. Raj, thanks for the opportunity again. I think this is going to be a great year. Winnie, I appreciate your control on the *Star Trek* jokes."

"I aim to please."

"Right. Okay, thanks, everyone. Enjoy the rest of your day." He gave Winnie a pointed look and then jerked his chin up at Raj as if he was bro-ing it out before he left, using the side aisle of the auditorium. Winnie turned to talk to Raj, but he was already grabbing his bag and bolting without a backward glance.

She sighed as she exited stage left and met Bridget in the aisle.

"That wasn't so bad," Bridget whispered. "You had such an awesome vibe going on, like you totally didn't care that he broke your heart on every social media site that ever existed."

"Bridget, what the hell *was* that? Raj looked so sad, and then he let me take over. And what's this whole thing with our new faculty advisor? Mr. Reece has *barely* tolerated me since I had him for homeroom teacher freshman year. He better not split up the festival and the film-club roles, because both have to be on my college application if I'm getting into NYU."

"Yeah, that's a game changer, isn't it?" Bridget said.

Dev Khanna stepped into Winnie's line of sight. He topped six feet, and he had beautiful dark skin and a lean frame. Something inside Winnie's stomach fluttered.

"What's the deal with Raj, the film-club traitor?" he asked, running a hand through his wavy hair. He locked eyes with Winnie. There was that strange click again. Some things from freshman year hadn't changed after all.

"Wow, right to the chase," Bridget said. "Isn't this the first time you've spoken directly to us in, like, ever? What gives, Tarantino?"

Dev shrugged. "It's the first time you guys aren't attached

at the hip to Raj. He's been a tool since high school started. Now you know that, too."

Winnie's phone buzzed in her pocket. She'd felt it go off during the meeting but hadn't had a moment to check. When she saw the slew of twenty-one text messages from her mother, she knew that facing the film club was just the beginning of her nightmare.

Dev peeked over her shoulder. "Looks like your mom's caps lock is stuck."

"Oh crap," Bridget said. "Your mom's texting you in caps? Do you think she found out? I told you it would backfire, Winnie."

For once, Winnie was speechless.

WINNIE COME HOME RIGHT NOW

YOU ARE NEVER ALLOWED TO LEAVE THE HOUSE AGAIN

WE ARE GOING TO SEND YOU TO BOARDING SCHOOL IN INDIA

THE NUNS IN INDIA WILL TAKE CARE OF YOU

HOW DARE YOU TRY TO RUIN THE FAMILY NAME????????????

IF YOU ARENT HOME IN TEN MINUTES IM CALLING
THE POLICE TO GET YOU AND THEN WE WONT BAIL
YOU OUT OF JAIL!!!!!!!!!!!!

"I feel like I'm missing something," Dev said.

"You are," Bridget said. "Winnie's mom is like a champion texter. She texts her friends all day and her family overseas. She knows very well how to use emojis, stickers, filters, GIFs, and especially caps lock. If she's texting Winnie in all caps, it means Winnie is dead meat."

"I gotta go," Winnie said. She had five minutes to get home, when it usually took fifteen. She was hoping that the threat of calling the police was subject to Indian Standard Time, which gave her an extra two hours.

She took her backpack from Bridget and slung it over one shoulder. "I'll see you tomorrow," she said, and brushed past Dev. Thinking about him had to wait, getting in touch with Raj had to wait, and, most importantly, film club had to wait. Right now, Winnie Mehta had to face the grand high executioner.

4

HUMPTY SHARMA KI DULHANIA /
HUMPTY SHARMA'S BRIDE
★★★★☆

Parents in Bollywood movies. Scary. Super scary, and sometimes super accurate. Other times . . . well, not so much.

After shifting her car into park in the middle of her driveway, Winnie ran to the front door and kicked off her shoes in the foyer. She heard her mother's voice from the kitchen.

"Vaneeta Mehta," she said in a clipped accent. *Uh-oh.* If Winnie's name sounded like a question, her mother wanted to know if she was hungry. If her name sounded like a command, then the gods were about to duck for cover.

"Just get it over with," she whispered to herself. "Like ripping off a Band-Aid."

Sita Mehta stood at the kitchen island, flipping rotis in a shallow pan. Her bangles jingled as her fingers moved deftly from raw dough to flour to rolling pin to stove.

Winnie's father, Deepak Mehta, sat at a bar stool across from her. His glasses were perched low on his nose as he read a finance magazine. He tapped his toe to the old Indian music coming through the speakers in the walls and ceilings. A slim remote sat at his elbow next to a cup of chai.

The kitchen was filled with the scent of fresh Indian bread and curried vegetables.

"Dinner already?" Winnie asked, putting on her best cutesy voice. Like that would help, she thought. She could tell by her mother's body language that she was in deep cow dung.

"Come here."

Winnie's father shot her a warning glance over the edge of his magazine but quickly looked down again.

Oh yeah. Deep, deep, *deep* cow dung. Her palms started sweating as she inched forward.

"What's . . . what's wrong?"

"What's wrong?" her mother replied sweetly. "I'll tell you what's wrong." She pinched dough from the mixing bowl and rolled it into a tiny ball in her hand. Then she slammed the ball down onto the counter in front of her.

"I got a call from Binnie Auntie, who got a call from Minnie Auntie, who got a text from Raj's mother, who was upset that someone took Raj's movies from his room while he wasn't home. That woman actually had the nerve to tell Minnie, who told Binnie, who said to me that they thought *my daughter* was the one who stole something!"

Winnie flinched as the rolling pin made a loud cracking sound when her mother dropped it onto the dough ball. She began pushing the ball into a thin, flat circle. Her father brushed some of the flying flour off the edge of his magazine page and kept reading.

"I told Binnie," her mother continued, "my daughter would never *steal* from someone. And besides, Raj may not be her boyfriend right now, but they've been destined to be together since they were children. They played with colored powder at our Indian Society Holi festival. They lit firecrackers on Diwali. I did the carpool with Chaya for years so they could ride to school together. There must be some misunderstanding, and that bowlegged, hook-nose, bad-hair-dye woman who buys her clothes from a secondhand trash store doesn't know what she's talking about."

Winnie prayed that her fear wasn't obvious. "Uh, thanks, Mom."

The rolling pin made another whacking sound against the counter, and her father's teacup rattled this time. She watched in admiration as he calmly lifted the cup and took a sip.

"Well, I thought that was the end of that conversation with Minnie—"

"Binnie."

"*Whatever.* But do you know what she told me?"

"Uh, no . . ."

"She said that Minnie told her that the Shahs' neighbor watched you, criminal-in-the-making, taking things out of Raj Shah's house. What do you have to say to that?"

"It could have been one of Raj's other girlfriends," Winnie said with a shrug. "According to Facebook, Twitter, Instagram, Tumblr, and Snapchat, we aren't together anymore."

"Vaneeta Mehta, do not lie to me! Did you steal from Raj Shah?"

Now that it had been a few days since she'd broken into Raj's house, she felt guilty for breaking and entering, but she couldn't do anything about it.

"Okay," she said, raising her hands, palms up. "Maybe I used the garage code I had and went to Raj's room to take some DVDs, but everything I took was stuff I bought for him. None of it was actually his in the first place. If you want me to apologize to Raj, fine. I'll do it, but I won't mean it."

Her dad snorted, and when her mother shot him a death stare—all big, wild eyes with thin lips—he buried his face in his reading material.

"Winnie, you've embarrassed me and your father in front of the whole Indian community. You know what respect is called in Hindi? *Izzat*. We lost the respect of our friends because of your behavior. Because you didn't think of anyone but yourself. How are we supposed to face Raj's parents in public now? You know we belong to the same Indian association. If it wasn't for this man, I'd send you to boarding school!" She pointed at Winnie's father with the rolling pin.

"Mom, the Indian community in Princeton, New Jersey, is like fifty thousand people who just happen to all be in your 'association.' I doubt everyone knows that I took my revenge. And besides, I have bigger problems to think about right now."

"What's bigger than stealing? You broke into their house, Winnie. You're lucky that Raj's parents haven't called the police. I can't even say my daughter was innocent because someone saw you. Do you know what they'll say to me now? That we are bad parents. At any party we go to from now on, they'll worry that I'll be sliding their Lenox flatware into my purse when the host isn't looking."

She resumed ranting, this time in Hindi and then in Punjabi, each word punctuated by wild hand gestures. Winnie linked her fingers together and waited from her spot in the middle of the kitchen. After a few more minutes, Sita Mehta quieted and slipped the last roti onto a plate before running a thin slab of ghee over it.

"I'm sorry I embarrassed you," Winnie said.

Her mother shut the stove off with a quick jerk of her wrist. "Tell me, what started all this? You two were destined to be together. Everyone saw it, even Pandit Ohmi."

"I may have asked for a break at the beginning of summer, but technically *he* broke up with *me* when I came back and found out he cheated. He's with someone else, and I don't want him anymore."

"But your future happiness relies on him, Winnie. We've been over your prophecy already. Don't ruin your chances."

"Nice, Ma," Winnie said, her voice dripping with sarcasm. "I should sacrifice happiness to be with someone who isn't right for me because you think he's my only hope. It's not as if I'm enjoying all of this. Remember, Raj was one of my best friends next to Bridget."

"He wants something different from his life, too," her father said. His soft voice ricocheted through the kitchen with more presence than her mother's tirade. "He wants money like his father now. Different path than film. You don't have much in common anymore."

"See? Even Dad knows that Raj went all Shashi Kapoor like in that Wall movie."

"*Deewaar*," her father said. "But it was Amitabh Bachchan who was focused on money. Shashi Kapoor was happy he had his family. His life was content and—"

"No!" Winnie's mother shouted. "You two don't even think about going off on one of your movie conversations right now. Winnie, you should've talked to Raj instead of stealing—"

"He wouldn't speak to me, Mom. Not even at film club. He isn't Pandit Ohmi's answer to my destiny. Not anymore. I know you really wanted that—I sort of wanted that, too—but we're not meant to be."

"Well, not if you don't try. Destiny needs to be believed in for it to come true."

The problem was that Winnie didn't want to believe in her destiny anymore. She knew arguing with her mother was useless. They were never going to see eye to eye on this issue. She dropped into one of the chairs at the kitchen table set with three place settings and a covered dish. Winnie grabbed the water jug and poured herself a glass.

Her mother put one roti and a serving of vegetables on her plate before pressing a kiss on the top of Winnie's head and settling down across from her. A moment later her father joined the table as well.

They ate for almost five full minutes before her father spoke. His tone was calmer than her mother's.

"Winnie, beta," he said. "You know this could have hurt your chances of getting into NYU."

"I know."

"And?"

"And my dream school is so much more important to me than revenge, but I needed to do this. To take back something of mine. Like every Ranbir Kapoor movie that ever existed."

Her father rolled his eyes. "I seem to recall that every Ranbir Kapoor movie was more about running away from problems instead of starting over."

"What? So not true!"

Winnie was about to launch into her list of examples when her mother brought her hand down like an ax.

"Fine," Winnie said. "But Dad's wrong."

"I'm never wrong. And if you don't think about getting into NYU first, you're going to lose what you've worked so hard for, before you even have a chance at it."

"Focusing on your future means focusing on your match,

too," her mother added. "It was practically handed to you on a silver thaali." She gestured like she was holding a platter up for Winnie. "Not all of us have the luxury of pursuing career and marriage equally."

Talk about added pressure. Her dad had given up film school to marry her mom because of the prophecy. A part of her wanted to get into film school for him as well. He never said anything about it, but if she could show him that she'd succeeded for both of them, maybe he'd feel as if he was getting his dream, too. Winnie remembered Pandit Ohmi's words and his assurance that her father would be proud of her regardless, but she still wasn't sure that was enough.

"This is the year we work on your college application," her father said.

"Yeah, early decision is coming up for NYU. If I get in, I can apply for the Yash Chopra Fellowship, the only one that deals with South Asian film theory. The first step is getting into college, though. I talked to Pandit Ohmi and—"

"You talked to Pandit Ohmi? When did this happen?" her mother said, her voice rising.

"A couple of days ago. Nani gave me his number."

"Winnie!"

"What?" Winnie shrugged. "I had to tell him to stop talking to you about my Bollywood romance janampatri because now that Raj dumped me, it's not going to happen."

"Winnie!" her parents said in unison.

"I didn't say it like *that*. I get that he's a pandit and all," she said, then paused to chew the last piece of roti. "Anyway, he had to know. Instead of agreeing, he told me that I was going to have these pitfalls in the next few months."

Her parents shared another look.

"She sounds like your mother," her father said.

"Our daughter is so *filmi* because you're the one who made her sit and watch all those old Amitabh Bachchan and Shah Rukh Khan movies every weekend. That's the only reason she's a drama queen—total nakhrewali. Speaking of my mother, she's coming next week to stay for a while."

"Nani is coming to stay?" Winnie asked with a squeal. Her grandmother was completely squealworthy.

"Hai Ram," her father said with a groan. "That means not only do I have to restock the Johnnie Walker, but we have to deal with our nakhrewali daughter before your mother decides to defend her." He spooned more vegetables onto his plate before giving Winnie a knowing look.

"What?"

"Your mother and I understand the significance of Pandit Ohmi's natal star-chart readings more than anyone. We lived it and had to face hard choices as well. But stealing, Winnie? It doesn't serve a point you're trying to make if you end up jeopardizing your future. You've never acted like this before, so we're not going to send you to boarding school like your mother wants. But you will give Raj his movies back."

"Uh, there may be a problem with that. . . ."

"What kind of a problem?"

"I may have buried them."

"*May* have buried them? As in in the ground?"

"Yes. In the ground. I could dig them up, but since it rained last night, I don't know how good they'd be. I also have to *find* them because I don't remember the exact location. . . . Daddy, it was the principle of the matter!"

Her father hung his head and said with a long-suffering sigh, "Then you'll repay Raj, giving him the money value of the property you took."

"Dad—"

"You and I both know what our movie collections mean to us. If Raj's held the same importance to him, and I'm sure it did if you gave it to him, then it's only right you pay him so he can rebuild his library. Your mother is right. It is about izzat."

"I used up all my money for film camp," Winnie said.

Her father grunted in acknowledgment.

"So, what, you want me to get a job even though you know I'm doing AP classes, college applications, the film club, and the film festival?"

"Yes."

"What about my review blog? That takes a lot of time."

Her dad looked at her blandly. "Your review site that no one reads?"

"Um, so not true."

"Your site talks only about the musicals. That's why no one reads it. You're not considering the new trends."

"Hey, just because I don't like new Bollywood with all its

kissing and lack of song-and-dance numbers doesn't mean my blog is outdated. Song-and-dance numbers are the pillars of the industry."

"Okay, enough, you two," her mother said. "Winnie, we can always have a pooja to pray for you to find your destined husband."

"No!" Winnie shouted. "Please do *not* invite your friends here to pray for me. That makes me look so pathetic." The thought of a prayer service with a gaggle of "aunties"—the women who hung out with her mother—all asking the gods to give her what she needed to find a man was nauseating.

"There is nothing wrong with a pooja," her mother said. She got up from the table, grabbed her dishes, and carried them to the sink. "You should be ashamed for saying that."

"Hey, praying is totally fine. It's the whole in-house pooja thing that drives me crazy. Daddy? No pooja. But a job?"

"You're working."

With a sigh she pushed her plate forward and dropped her head onto her folded arms. She mumbled into the crease of her elbow, "Where am I supposed to find a job that hires high school students? The summer season is over. Fall is, like, dead."

"The movie theater."

She jerked up. "Which movie theater? The one on Route 1? The one on Route 27? The one off 287? Do you mean the dine-in theater? The one in Bridgewater, or the one in Edison?"

"If you know something, just tell her," Winnie's mother said over the sound of running water.

"The Rose Theater," her father said. "You know my friend Eric, who owns it? I can ask him if he's hiring."

"The Rose?" She thought about the small art house that played independent movies on Nassau Street in downtown Princeton. She knew Henry worked there, at least in the summer, and some of the other film-club members had interned there. She'd never had time to work in a theater because she'd always interned elsewhere. But now? Clocking hours at the Rose would be awesome. For a steady paycheck, it was a great place to start.

She scratched at her bare wrist while she worked through her schedule in her head. The next few months would definitely suck no matter how awesome her job was going to be.

"Okay. I'll play along and be like Shammi Kapoor in *Professor*. I'll get a job under pretenses to pay off a debt."

Her father huffed. "I don't know how NYU is going to let you in with your movie references. There are at least ten other films that have a more comparable story line than that one. Shammi Kapoor had to play a role for a noble cause. There is nothing noble about your actions. And don't even think about doing something like this again. Understood?"

"Yeah, Dad."

"You overcomplicate everything," Winnie's mother said as she wiped down the counter. "Just accept what is."

Winnie nodded, but she refused to accept destiny at face

value anymore. She wanted to make the choices in her life, and nothing and nobody was going to tell her differently. She was sure that by her birthday in January, once she had confirmed proof that her prophecy was a lie, she'd be done with the bracelet, with Raj, and with anything that had to do with her star chart.

"You're going to be fine, beta." Her father helped dry the dishes while Winnie packed the leftovers. After a beat he added, "So how many DVDs did you bury?"

Winnie burst into laughter while her mother shook her head. She'd never admit it, but she had to have the most awesome Indian parents that a girl could ask for.

5

RAM LAKHAN
★★★★☆

You know the heroine is going to forgive the hero for leaving her (even temporarily) before it even happens. She sings an entire song about how brokenhearted she is, and when he comes back into her life, it's like, Yay! I knew we'd be together again! Ugh.

WINNIE: We need to talk, Raj.

WINNIE: I don't know why you're avoiding me, but if we're going to work together . . .

WINNIE: Seriously, what the hell, Raj????

When final bell rang, signaling the start of the weekend, Winnie was only stopped once in the hallway, an improvement from the rest of the week.

"How are you taking it?" Simone asked. "You know, the breakup?"

"Uh, I'm fine, actually."

"Well, if you ever want a breakup playlist, I can hook you up. I'll even ask some of the girls from—"

"That's really okay. Thanks, though. See you at the next meeting!"

She hustled toward Mr. Reece's office, ignoring the side-eye glances. She let out a sigh of relief when she finally reached his door. She knocked twice on the doorjamb and peeked through the opening.

"Hi, do you have a minute?" Winnie said when she saw him sitting behind his desk.

"Ms. Mehta, yes, have a seat. I'm almost finished."

Winnie slipped into one of the torn leather padded chairs facing Mr. Reece. She watched as he squinted at his computer, his shoulders hunched and his fingers hovering over a keyboard. Behind him was a large *Star Trek: The Next Generation* poster next to one of *The Big Bang Theory*. In the far corner were two physics gravity models. Nothing in his office paid tribute to the film club. That was annoying, Winnie thought.

"And done," Mr. Reece said with a click of his mouse. He leaned back in his chair, folding his hands together. "It's a little odd not having you in a class this year, but at least we have the film club. How are you feeling now that the first week of school is over?"

"Honestly, or should I give you the short, fake answer?"

Mr. Reece's forehead creased. "Honesty. Always honesty."

Winnie thought about it for a moment; then words started rushing from her mouth. "Okay, there is this one Bollywood movie called *Sholay* that my parents make me watch every Thanksgiving. It's like a tradition. After our tandoori turkey, we sit down with the family and literally quote the movie as it's playing. In the story, two con artists with really good hearts come to this small village to help an old man complete his plot for revenge."

"Ms. Mehta—"

"Hear me out. One of the con artists professes his love for Basanti, this loud-mouthed, independent village girl. Basanti's aunt is so not okay with this guy, so Con Artist gets super drunk, climbs a water tower, and threatens to jump unless Basanti's aunt lets him marry Basanti. The whole town is yelling at him to not jump, and then also yelling at Basanti's aunt to say yes to the marriage and to save his life."

"I'm not sure I'm following—"

Winnie planted her hands on the desk and leaned forward. "The film club is the town, Mr. Reece. They're watching me while someone has rejected me, and I'm begging Raj, who is Basanti, to pay attention. The only difference between me and the con artist in *Sholay* is that the town has no interest in helping me and I'm not drunk."

"Stop right there," Mr. Reece said, holding up a hand. "If this is you tattling on Raj, then I don't want to hear it. You two are young adults and can work through your own differences."

"In all the years we've known each other, Mr. Reece, have I ever not acted like an adult? My life is *Sholay* right now. I need an Amitabh Bachchan."

"A who?"

"The other con man in the story. Amitabh doesn't exactly *say* that he's helping, and as a front, it looks like he made the situation worse by telling the aunt some bad stuff. But everyone who has ever watched the movie knows that Amitabh has a key part in his con-man friend's happiness. I need you to help convince Raj to talk to me. Subtly. Like Amitabh."

"You'll figure it out between the two of you, Winnie. Or Raj will. He seems to be doing a great job with not only communicating the film-club lineup, but everything else."

"What? I *made* that lineup last year when I gave it to Ms. Jackson!"

"Raj shared it with me and walked me through it, something you should've handled instead of hassling Ms. Jackson to come back. Raj has many other commitments, and yet he's executing the work for the club and festival—"

"Thanks to *me*," Winnie said.

"Be that as it may . . . Raj is doing a bang-up job. He's even taking the initiative of finding a festival headliner, which you've never thought to do."

Winnie felt as if Mr. Reece had slapped her across the face. "I'm sorry, I have no idea what you're talking about. What headliner?"

Mr. Reece sighed. "Instead of inviting the same judges we do every year, he wants to get someone with a little bit more clout using his father's new connections. I know you're butting heads with him, but a headliner could generate revenue for the club. It's also in the bylaws as an option for club events."

"The reason our judges are the same at the film festival every year is because Princeton University gives us the auditorium for *free* if we support their film and drama department. That's a huge expense we don't have to cover with the fund-raiser. But if we need to pay for a location, the amount of money we have to raise goes up by almost five thousand dollars. We don't have that much cash, which means we won't have a *venue*."

"I suggest you lower your voice, Ms. Mehta," he said. "I think you need to appreciate your current role. You're still leading the weekend club events. You sent the correspondence for this Sunday evening's viewing. From what I can tell, Raj let you take charge of that while he handles the festival, like it should be. This isn't a competition."

"But it's becoming one," she said. "It feels like he's edging me out of the film festival and you're helping. I—I still have feelings," she said, her voice hitching. "Like a leftover friendship thing, maybe, and you're not making this easy for me to deal with while I'm trying to build my college application."

Mr. Reece's eyes widened in alarm. "Hold it. Crying is for the counselor's office." He pulled out a dozen tissues from the box on his desk and shoved them toward her.

Winnie picked up one from the pile and sniffled into it. "Okay." She wanted to add *jerk* but knew that would be pushing it.

"I think you better sit down with Raj, Winnie," Mr. Reece said gently. "You can't run to the faculty advisor for everything. That may have been how Ms. Jackson managed it, but not me. Let me know what you decide."

He looked at her as if he was waiting for her to leave, so with the little bit of pride she had left, Winnie grabbed her backpack and ticked two fingers against her forehead in a salute.

"Well, I learned that I may be standing on a water tower," she said, sniffling one last time, "but I don't have anyone's support today. Thanks for being so incredibly helpful, Mr. Reece. You are definitely not an Amitabh Bachchan."

"Ms. Mehta—"

She was already shutting the door behind her and walking toward the nearest exit. When she rounded a corner, she saw a very familiar head.

The hallways cleared for Raj as he walked down the corridor. It was almost as if people were making way for royalty. Winnie rushed toward him, ignoring the crowd, who obviously didn't treat her the same way. When she got to the door he'd passed through, her stomach dropped. The boys' bathroom. Great.

Should she wait for him?

No, she thought. This was her only chance. Holding her fear like Nargis held farming equipment in *Mother India,* she opened the door.

"Raj?" she called out.

"What the hell?" Raj said, yanking at his zipper. His words accompanied the sound of a flush. "What are you *doing* in here?"

She locked the door with one sweaty hand. "I came from Mr. Reece's office, and he said that I had to make you listen, so I guess we're going to talk here."

He took a step toward her. "I need to—"

"Stop right there." She planted herself, legs spread, in front of the door. "I have something to say to you. How is it that your entire fan club knows that you've broken up with me, but I had to assume since you won't tell me to my face?"

He flinched. "You broke up with me before you left."

"I asked for a break, not a breakup—"

"A break means we broke up. You pulled a Sarah Marshall on me."

"No way! You were the Sarah Marshall, since you went off to be with someone else. You were a great boyfriend and I thought maybe we could see what happened when school started, but now you won't even freaking *talk* to me."

"Winnie, do you even listen to yourself?" He flung his hands out, his eyes wide. "Do you see what you're doing right now?" He motioned to the pale blue tiled walls and urinals. "You take my movies—"

"Only the ones I bought you, and my parents are making me pay for them since I don't remember where I buried them."

"—and then you bust in here!"

"I'm doing this because the film club and the film festival are important to my future even though they aren't important to yours anymore."

"That's because even though I love you, I grew up, Winnie!" he shouted.

The bathroom filled with silence.

"I grew up," he said again, this time more softly. "Bollywood is not a way of life. It's an industry, a career, and it doesn't make good money. This fantasy dreamland you live in doesn't exist. It took me a long time to realize that. That's why I'm going to a different school, and doing different things. That's what I asked you to consider at the beginning of the summer. No matter how much you love movies, I thought you'd be more practical and realize that your love for movies . . . is a hobby."

Winnie wiped away the tear that traced the curve of her cheek. His words stabbed her heart. She'd never thought that Raj believed the one thing she loved to do more than anything in the world wasn't worthy of a career.

"How could you have ever been the one for me if you didn't believe in me? I'm glad we aren't together anymore, because I expect more from my boyfriend."

"Winnie, I'm trying to be a little realistic here—"

"No. You're giving up. Why are you even in film club if you feel that way about movies?"

He shoved his hands in his pockets. "I need the credit for my college application," he murmured.

"What! What did you say?" She wanted to barrel her fist into his stomach. "We used to hate people who joined film club for credit."

"No, *you* hated people who joined for credit, and I just agreed with you because it was easier than telling you not to make such a big deal out of it."

"So you lied to me? Did you lie about believing in the prophecy, too?"

"What? No! I did everything I could to convince you that we were destined to be together like we were told when we were kids. I bought you that bracelet your parents kept talking about. Isn't that proof enough that I tried to make this work?"

Winnie clamped her trembling hands on his shoulders. "Buying me a bracelet doesn't make me believe in you, any more than it makes you believe in me. I've held on to it for a week because I needed time to process what happened between us, but now I know I have to give it back. First, I want to hear you say it. That you're the one breaking up with me. Reading it on Facebook doesn't count."

"I . . . can't."

"Why?"

He closed his eyes and leaned his forehead against hers. She shuddered at the contact: the cool sensation of his skin was so familiar, but hazy like a distant memory.

"Because I missed you," he whispered. "As crazy as you are, I missed you. Watching you during the meeting this week, looking at you now, I still have hope."

"But you're with Jenny now." She stepped back, rubbing her damp palms against her jeans. The words coming out of Raj's mouth didn't make any sense.

"Yeah. Jenny is different. She's . . . not the firestorm you are. I needed to be with someone like that to understand what I had with you. I'm so sorry I hurt you, Winnie. I'm realizing the mistake I made. Maybe subconsciously I thought you would see Jenny and me together and—"

"No." Winnie cleared her throat. This couldn't be happening right now. She had to get this script back on track. "Stay with Jenny. You've changed, and I'm still the same. Let's try to make things work for the film club, which means answering my messages, okay? Also, Reece told me you're trying to get some special judge for the film festival. What's up with that?"

"Oh. Well, even though I don't think a future in film is the best way to go, I wanted your last year to be special."

She paused. "Okay. Okay, that's . . . nice. I wish you'd talked to me, though. I—I'm okay with new things, but we have to edit the website, the ads, the promo stuff. We have to clear it with Princeton University, too. It could totally screw things up with securing the location—"

"Don't worry, I've already brought it all up to Mr. Reece. This is going to be great. I promise you'll love it. I'm doing this for you."

"Raj, how many times do I have to remind you that you're dating Jenny Dickens?"

"Jenny has been amazing at a time when I needed someone like her. But you and I? Bracelet or not, we have history. Keep the bracelet, Winnie. The more I think about you, the more I know I made a mistake letting you go so easily."

A knot of dread tightened in her stomach. "You think we can still work. After you cheated, and even though you think what I want in life is stupid. Raj . . . you still think I should go to Boston, don't you?"

"You'll realize soon enough," he said. He kissed the corner of her mouth. "Like I said—I love you. After this summer, after seeing you this week and especially now, I know we're still destined. I was giving you space. Maybe you still need some space to come to terms with your future."

"If you really loved me, then you'd want me to get into NYU."

"You know what I think?"

"What?"

"I think you are making excuses because after watching all those movies, you don't know how to be practical," he said, before pushing through the door.

She tried to follow him and give one last parting shot, but someone blocked her. Dev Khanna filled the entrance. He maneuvered her inside and locked the door behind him.

"What are you—"

"I'm saving you from the crowd of people in the hall," he said as he leaned against the far wall. With a bored expression, he started scrolling through something on his phone.

"Why'd you lock the door?"

"Um, so no one can come in?" he replied. "You can leave now, but chances are they'll know you were in here with Shah."

"Wait, did you . . ."

"Yup. My locker is right outside the bathroom door. I was trying to fix my broken lock and ended up hearing everything. By the way, don't feel bad. Dude was a jerk trying to get you to think you were wrong about your future. Also, he's a total moron for letting you go. You deserve way better."

"Hey!" She could feel her cheeks redden. *Hey?* Really, that was all she could respond with?

"What? That was a compliment." He looked up from his phone, and when their eyes met, the corner of Dev's mouth curved slowly, as if he knew what she was thinking.

"You have no filter, you know that?" she said.

"And you have no common sense."

"Is that supposed to be a compliment, too?"

He laughed, and the sound was enough to make her toes curl.

"Someone's gotta make sure you're thinking straight when Raj obviously wants you back. You know you can't go there, right?"

"Oh yeah? Why not?"

He grinned, combing his fingers through his hair. "He's the kind of guy who sells puppies and kittens for a profit and makes you believe it's for a good cause. Besides. You've said nice stuff about my work, so I'm happy to help you get over douchebag traitor."

"Uh, thanks? You're good at what you do. The best film student in the school. Stuff is a little dark, but everyone knows you're going places."

"Thanks."

"You're welcome. So, did anyone else—"

"Don't worry, no one else could hear you guys. Did you actually expect to still work together?"

Before she could answer, the door rattled. Winnie jumped back, and heard muffled voices followed by the sound of retreating footsteps.

"I don't know," she said after a moment. "I had no game plan."

"Well, you better get one soon." Dev came closer, reached past her shoulder, and flipped open the lock. His eyes stayed on hers as he slowly opened the door, brushing her arm. Winnie jerked in surprise at the contact, which only made him smile.

Dev stuck his head into the hallway, looked both ways, and stepped aside. "Coast is clear."

Winnie was down the hall, heart pounding, before Dev caught up with her.

They made it to the exit door, and Dev stepped in front of her, pushing it open so she could walk through. In that one moment, she was framed in the doorway with him again.

Click.

She stumbled down the front steps.

"Thanks for the help," she called out as she headed to her car.

"Winnie!"

She turned. "Yeah?"

"If it came down to either you or him for the club, I'd vote for you," he said. "Not because I hate your ex, but because you're the best for the job. I'll even step in as one of those Bollywood types and save you from the villainous Raj."

She laughed. "Indian movie references are obviously not your thing, but there is something you should know about me if we're going to talk more often than we have in the last three years."

"Oh yeah? What's that?"

"As much as I love Bollywood damsels in distress, I don't need saving. I'm my own hero." She flipped her hair over her shoulder. It was a flirt move and such a cliché line, but he'd given her an opening, and any self-respecting film buff would've taken it. She felt him watching her the whole time she walked to her car.

Winnie reversed from the parking lot, glancing at the front of the school. When she spotted the empty stoop, she sighed. She didn't expect him to watch her leave, so she really couldn't be disappointed that he hadn't hung around.

She turned onto one of the roads that led straight to her house before calling Bridget through her Bluetooth.

"Where did you go?" Bridget said when she answered.

"We need to have a team huddle. I have a story to tell you. Oh! And a weird dream we really need to discuss."

"A full-blown huddle or a mini one?"

"Full-blown."

"Okay," Bridget said. "I'll bring the ice cream. Bollywood movie?"

"I can't believe I'm saying this, but my life is getting a little too Indian dramatic, so let's do one of your picks."

"*Say Anything*?"

"The number of times I've watched that movie is insane, but yeah, that's okay."

"Awesome. I have a thing with my folks tonight, but let's do Saturday."

"You're on. Later."

Winnie disconnected and tried to stop replaying the last half hour in her head like a broken reel. Mr. Reece. Raj. Dev.

Indian heroines always screwed up when they tried to balance logic with emotion, so why was she trying to do the same thing?

Holy baby Shah Rukh Khan, her life was so majorly complicated.

6

NAMASTEY LONDON
★★☆☆☆

Bollywood doesn't do enough to show that women have jobs. I'd like to see one Katrina Kaif movie where not only is she employed in a corporate office, but she actually WORKS. Lunching doesn't count.

When Winnie finally surfaced on Sunday after Bridget left, sleepy eyed, from their twelve-hour movie marathon, she found her father drinking chai at the kitchen counter and sitting in front of a laptop.

"Rough night?" he asked.

"We were brainstorming on how to combat Raj's weirdness." She gave him a hug. "You're watching *Namak Halaal*?" she asked when she saw his screen. "Dad!"

"What?"

"Why are you watching without me? And why aren't you watching on the TV?"

"Your mother won't let me watch on the big screen, and you weren't awake."

"Mom thinks you've seen it too many times." Winnie took a sip from his cup and then pulled up a stool next to him.

"Get your own chai," he grumbled. "Aren't you going to go to the movie theater today?"

"Yeah. Do I need to dress up? Any time I go, no one is dressed up."

He shrugged. "I don't think so. People don't wear suits and dresses to a movie theater."

Winnie watched the movie with her dad for a few minutes. When a song-and-dance number started, she asked, "Do you regret it, Daddy? Not being in Bombay? Not working in movies like you wanted?"

"No. Never," he said.

"Really?"

He nodded. "How can I ever regret something when the choices I've made have produced something so much greater than I could've accomplished on my own?" He pinched Winnie's chin.

Winnie kissed his cheek. "I'm going to tell Mom you've been sneaking her ginger-root tea bags if you watch this without me again."

"Hey!" he said, but she was already out the door.

Winnie considered her father's answer all the way into downtown Princeton. Would she give up her love for Bollywood and a career in film studies because of something a priest said to her about a potential happily-ever-after? She didn't think it was possible.

Pondering her father's love story naturally progressed to reflecting on Pandit Ohmi, and her strange Bollywood dreams. She couldn't ignore their significance to her current situation. Maybe Shah Rukh Khan manifested because she hadn't gotten a chance to give the bracelet back to Raj. Holding on to it could give him the impression that she still had hope. In all truthfulness, she believed her star chart could come true; that would take some time to get over. But she knew her relationship with Raj was done.

When she stopped in front of the Rose Theater, she noticed that the shutters were pulled over the ticket windows and a CLOSED sign hung over the entrance, but when she tested the door, it swung open. She looked around at the busy street before stepping inside.

"Hello?" Recessed lighting brightened the short glass cabinet along the left wall of the empty lobby. "Is anybody here?"

"Hi."

Winnie whirled to face the voice. *"Dev?"*

"The one and only," he said. "What are you doing here? First you're stalking your ex, now me?"

"What? No! Never. I mean, why would I stalk you?"

He grinned. "I don't know. Maybe it's because you finally realized we're meant to be?"

"Sorry, Romeo," Winnie said with a laugh. "Destiny and I are not getting along right now."

"Damn. Okay, then what brings you to the Rose?"

"Forget me—what are *you* doing here?"

"I work here."

"Really? Since when?"

"Since the beginning of summer. What, is that really so hard to believe?"

"No, it's just that I didn't expect Mr. Tall, Dark, and . . . uh, *you* to get a job at the Rose. My father knows the owner, Eric, so I was able to get an interview."

"Yeah? Eric mentioned that he had one or two spots open. Henry and I thought they'd go to college students."

"I know Henry is the tech guy. He's always the tech guy. But what do you do here?"

"I run the ticket booth most of the time, but I also order new films. It's a pretty cool gig. This job funds my camera collection. Come on, I'll introduce you to Eric. Hopefully, you can join the crew. It wouldn't be such a bad thing seeing you around, Winnie Mehta. You're the only other person I know who has an encyclopedic brain when it comes to movies."

"Is that a bad thing?"

He grinned. "No. It's a great thing."

Keep it together, Mehta, she chanted even as she felt a shiver rush up her spine. It was a sensation she had never experienced with Raj, which she realized both alarmed and thrilled her at the same time.

Dev led her down a narrow hall and knocked on the open door at the end. "Eric? Your new recruit is here. I can vouch for her. She runs the film festival at school."

A burly, balding man sat behind a metal desk piled with stacks of paper. "Winnie? Welcome! Come in, come in. Oh my goodness, you look just like your father."

"Hi," she said as she shook his hand. "I've heard that one before."

She turned, ignored Dev's curious expression, shut the office door in his face, and slipped into one of the metal chairs. It took only a moment for Eric to start firing questions, first about her interest in movies, and then about her understanding of film.

Yes, she had a blog where she reviewed movies. Yes, she knew Hollywood, foreign, and Bollywood, but Bollywood was her favorite. Yes, she'd learned 35-mm film at film camp.

"I'm a purist," Eric said, pressing a hand to his wide chest. "We keep thirty-five-millimeter film projectors to play the classics and art-house movies. I'm the only one who knows how to splice film, but it's taking up too much of my time. I need a projectionist who can stay up in the room with the machines, and splice and thread the film to prep the projectors a few times a week."

"I can definitely be your projection-room tech," Winnie said. "I love working with film. I learned how to do it this summer, and I can splice and build a movie faster than it takes Scorsese to kill a character."

Eric laughed. "I trust your father, so I'm sure you'll be fine, but why don't you show me what you've got? I want to see for myself that I can trust you with my film."

"Sure. Works for me."

In the lobby, Dev was unboxing candy.

"Where are you going?"

"Winnie's going to show me her film-splicing ability. Want to see?"

Dev pocketed the knife and followed them to the second floor.

In the cool, dim room, Winnie walked over to the makeup table and switched it on. "Ready?" she said.

"I'm not going to time you," Eric said with a smile.

"Right," she said. She waited for the table to warm up before she started to put the strips of film together. She was careful with the old *Casablanca* practice reel he passed her and quickly built the movie lead. She then threaded the lead onto the platters and soundhead assembly. She ran a hand over the framing knob and film shoe, positioning the film into the machine. She deftly formed a proper loop with the film.

Eric stood next to her, arms crossed. "Not bad. Not bad at all. It takes someone who really appreciates film to do this. Even people who host flash screenings claim to appreciate movies, but they don't get it."

"Flash screenings? You guys get requests for them here? I thought that was only big in the city."

"Yeah, the college crowd likes it," Dev said. "Art-house film screenings with only twenty-four hours' notice to the public create a lot of buzz. The spontaneity brings people in the door. We've actually had to turn some business down because of all the requests recently." He kicked the base of one of the platters.

"That's a shame," Winnie said. "But I splice pretty quickly, so maybe you can show more movies with two people putting film together." After cutting the lights, she listened to the telltale hum of the shifting strips.

Dev leaned forward as the images played across the screen. "You're definitely surprising, Winnie Mehta," he said.

"And accurate, too," Eric added. "You want the job?"

"Yeah, absolutely."

"Great! Then let's get you set up with all the paperwork. You're going to love this place."

Winnie tried to control the skip in her step as they headed toward the office. She sat across from Eric and started filling out her application, when she felt her phone vibrate. She peeked at Bridget's message.

Emergency!!!

She quickly put her phone away. Not good.

"Is something wrong?" Eric asked.

"What? Oh no. Nope, not at all." She rushed through the rest of the documents and handed them to Eric.

"Welcome to the team," he said. "I'll set up your schedule tonight and send it to you."

"Thanks. I'm excited. I'll see you soon."

Winnie was almost through the front door before Dev caught up with her.

"Whoa, wait a minute. What's going on?"

She held up her phone. "Bridget's been messaging me." She looked down at the screen.

Emergency!!!

Call ASAP!!!

Wher r u????

Her phone slipped from her hand and dropped to the carpet when she finished reading the messages.

Before she could pick it up, Dev was there, doing it for her.

"Raj got *who* for the film festival?"

She snatched the phone back. "It's a joke, right? It has to be a joke. I mean, Gurinder Chadha. *Bend It Like Beckham* and *Bride and Prejudice*. Writer, director, and producer. Raj knows she's my hero. I have no idea how he pulled this off." She fanned herself as she went a little light-headed.

"Like I said, he wants you back," Dev said.

"I'm getting that."

"Well, this is not an Eddie Murphy movie from the

eighties about a golden child with bad guys and ancient prophecies."

"Shows what you know."

Meeting Gurinder Chada was a once-in-a-lifetime opportunity, and if it was true, then her life just became even more surreal.

"I gotta leave."

"Okay. Winnie? Try to remember that he probably has an ulterior motive."

Winnie didn't know how to respond to that, so she waved and ran to her car. After buckling in, she checked her phone again. Maybe Bridget had heard wrong. If Raj was smart, he'd post the news on his old movie-review site.

Wrinkling her nose at his last movie review, which was seriously off by at least two stars, she scrolled through his events page. There, in black-and-white print, Raj had included Gurinder Chadha's bio. She was attending the Princeton Academy Student Film Festival.

Winnie squealed so loudly the couple walking past her car stared.

She sent Bridget two screens of emojis before she texted Raj.

WINNIE: When you said you'd find a guest judge, I didn't think you'd get my hero. This is amazing!!!
RAJ: Did it for you.

WINNIE: . . .

WINNIE: Or the film club. Bc you still love it and want to do something with movies.

RAJ: LMAO. No this is all connections. I bet the guy in your prophecy would do the same thing for you. Right???

WINNIE: Maybe? Did you tell Reece?

RAJ: Oh. Yeah. Listen, about that . . . don't be mad. I'm fixing it so don't panic when you read his email.

That was not a good sign. "What did you do, Raj?" she muttered as she checked her messages for the note from Mr. Reece. She opened it up, and all the euphoria and shock she felt was immediately replaced with horror.

To: Vaneeta Mehta
From: Mr. William Reece
Subject: Film Festival Chair

Please see me before the meeting. Shouldn't take long. In the auditorium is fine.

Mr. Reece

She was a straight-A student, and she knew how to read between the lines. Mr. Reece was going to give Raj the festival to run. She was going to officially be pushed out of the role. She'd have to smile at the club film screening tonight, as if nothing was wrong, and wait until their meeting tomorrow to learn the final verdict.

Winnie had struggled for years to set herself up for a future at one of the best film schools in the country. Now that she was so close to proving herself, it was as if someone was patting her on the head and telling her, "Thanks, but no thanks." She knew that she was super driven, and that she could get tunnel vision about following her dreams, but she couldn't help being so passionate about movies. It was part of who she was. And now she was torn. On the one hand, she'd get to meet a role model. And on the other, there was a good chance she wouldn't get into the school she'd always imagined she'd attend. She'd live an ordinary life instead of the extraordinary one that she'd always hoped for.

Winnie drove home with her emotions swinging in every direction. After she pulled into the driveway, she slipped out of the car and through the front door. The whole house was perfumed with rich scents of spices. Music played in the kitchen and echoed in the entranceway.

"Winnie?" her mother called. "Your nani has arrived! Come here."

Winnie didn't respond as she yanked off her Converses.

"Beta?" Her mother entered the front foyer, holding a wooden spoon in one hand. She was wearing the pale pink salwar kameez she usually wore around the house. "What's wrong?"

Winnie lost her cool like a Bollywood heroine who was just told that her life was doomed. The only difference was that Winnie couldn't control her mascara from bleeding all over her face as she ugly-cried.

"Raj got Gurinder Chadha as the guest of honor for the film festival, and I'm so happy for the festival but so mad because it'll be practically impossible for me to get into NYU, and I'll end up with this stupid prophecy that won't come true while working at the theater forever, and I don't like being a defeatist but I feel like I lost and I'm not even hormonal!"

"Oh, beta," her mother said soothingly. She opened her arms and Winnie stepped into them, rested her head on her mother's shoulder, and wailed. She'd cried more in the last week and a half than she had in the last year, but maybe things had been too easy for her, and her luck had run out.

As she was rocked in the softest of arms, Winnie knew that she'd somehow work through this. After all, her mom was there to help now that the only thing left to do with her broken dream was to pick up the pieces.

7

Winnie's mom set a cup of chai on the kitchen table along with a plate of cake rusk to dip in the hot liquid. Winnie huddled over the milky tea infused with cardamom and inhaled deeply, while her grandmother stood at her left, rubbing her arm.

"I'm s-s-sorry I'm a mess just when you g-got here, Nani," Winnie said. She had spent the last ten minutes venting while her grandmother and mother patiently listened.

"Bechari," the older woman said. "My poor girl." Nani's mint-green pants and mint-green velvet-lined top smelled like incense and India, which was an added comfort. Winnie leaned into the soft velvet and took a breath. It made her feel a little better.

"You know what? I can call Raj's mother right now,"

Winnie's mom said. "I'll tell her to straighten her boy out. He should've known what this would do to your plans."

"Mom, p-please don't. That would be even more embarrassing. Especially since he's not doing anything wrong."

"That cow woman doesn't know how to raise her own children. I never liked her. And she thinks she is constantly dressed for a Miss India pageant now that she has money. Did you see her at temple last time? So gaudy."

Winnie tried for a shaky smile. "That won't do anything. Instead of being the cheating ex, Raj is trying to be the hero, even though he still hasn't apologized for cheating. How am I supposed to hate him when he did something nice and it's Mr. Reece who's messing up my future? Stupid rules."

Her mother said to Nani, "Maybe if they were together, this wouldn't have happened. He wants her back, you know."

"Mom, that's not—"

Nani let out a soft "oh ho." "Samajh aaya. I got it. He wants to be your destiny, but you don't want him to be. He's doing this nice thing for you, but it's made things worse for your college application so you *still* believe he's not your destiny. My poor bacha. I'm so sorry he's not the one for you anymore."

"She doesn't know that yet," her mom said over her shoulder as she went to the stove. She picked up a large wooden ladle to stir the contents of her stockpot.

"She knows," Nani said. "She told us with her own mouth. If my granddaughter cries with sadness when her old boyfriend tries to surprise her, don't you think he doesn't know how to make her happy? But, Winnie, your mother is right, too. Pandit Ohmi gave you everything you need to know, and you still manage to make things so confusing."

"Well, I don't expect you to get it, Nani. Your generation is old-fashioned enough to believe that Pandit Ohmi is one hundred percent right."

"Don't be calling me old. Next time I'll be whopping you with my chappal."

Winnie looked down to see if her grandmother was wearing sandals. Even with cataracts, her grandmother had killer aim. She could hit any target with one of her chappals. Thankfully she was barefoot today.

"Beta," her mother said. "You have to promise me you'll be open to having Raj in your life again."

"Can't you for once see how he's not the one for me and take my side?"

Her grandmother stroked her hair. "I can pray that after this is done he becomes a roach in his next life."

Winnie coughed. "Thanks, Nani, but yeah. Not helpful."

Nani leaned back in her chair. "Okay, maybe we can come up with another solution that doesn't involve Raj to get this Mr. Reece to see that you're important to the club."

"Ma, don't get her into any trouble," Winnie's mom said. "She already has to work to pay for taking Raj's movies."

The older woman's eyes sparkled. "Yes, I heard. Good job, beta."

"Muma!" Winnie's mother cried.

Winnie interrupted before her mother could start arguing with Nani. "I don't even want to go to school tomorrow. What am I supposed to say to everyone? 'Yeah, Raj did a great job finding Gurinder Chadha. I'm excited to meet her and just as excited to be kicked out of the festival.' This is worse than Raj dumping me for Jenny Dickens."

"You've mentioned to me more than once that Raj is dating another girl," her mother said with a raised eyebrow.

"What? Mom, that's not the point—"

"It could be. Either way, you have to go to school tomorrow to find out. I didn't raise a coward."

"I know, but, Mom—"

"Oh, don't give me that American 'but, Mom' attitude. You're Indian. You face this drama. It's in your dhadkan, your heartbeat."

"And like every other Indian," Nani said with a twinkle in her eye, "you create some more drama as a distraction." She saluted Winnie with her glass, which she'd picked up off the kitchen table. It had a pineapple wedge perched on the rim.

Winnie sighed. "I don't want more drama. I just want all this to disappear. And anyway, it feels like Raj is so much better at this stupid drama stuff than I am."

"Winnie, it sounds like you need to understand what you want first so you can tell Raj clearly that his actions are hurting you, no matter how well intentioned they are. Then, after that, you'll know how to talk to him about sharing the film-festival responsibilities."

"I don't even know where to start. I accepted Pandit Ohmi's prediction as truth for so long that I have no idea what I want instead of what I've been told I should want."

"It doesn't have to be that hard for you," Nani asked. "Is there someone else who is making Raj's interference seem confusing?"

"No way," Winnie said, even though Dev's face popped into her mind.

"Oh? That was very adamant," her grandmother mused.

Winnie busied herself with pulling at the ends of her hair. There was no way she was going to respond to that comment.

"Maybe your movies will give you the answer," Winnie's mother said. "Go and clean up. You'll come up with something before school tomorrow."

Winnie nodded, thinking that watching some Bollywood would be a good way to clear her head. She kissed her grandmother first, then her mother, and with one last wave over her shoulder, she headed upstairs.

She was feeling better about her situation, even though she knew she'd be back to dealing with a constant roiling nausea when school started the next morning. Until then, she could binge on something good and then head to the Sunday film-club showing. Winnie debated checking her online library, but her classic disc collection called her name. She scanned the boxes displayed on the floor-to-ceiling bookcases, which framed a TV in the middle of the wall unit. After choosing one of her favorites from the sixties, she flopped on her bed and picked up her phone. First things first, she thought.

"Hey, Bridge? Thanks for the heads-up."

"What are you going to do?" Bridget said on the other end of the phone.

"I'll see Mr. Reece and then grovel. There is nothing else I *can* do."

"What about Raj? If he's still with Jenny, then he's as much of a douche as I imagined. Now everyone's going to expect you and Raj to make up."

"Except for Dev Khanna," Winnie said. "I ran into him today and he didn't have very friendly thoughts toward Raj. He works at the Rose, apparently. Small world, right?"

"The Rose? Henry didn't mention that Dev worked with him. You have to admit that he's got that brooding artsy type down. He's like Raj's opposite. And the best part is that he has nothing to do with that prophecy of yours. Hey, maybe that's what you need. A break from some fantasy. Spend some time with him."

"My mom thinks I should still give Raj a chance. So basically, she said the opposite."

"Well, I think she's wrong. You guys look like you'll fit together."

Winnie thought of the click she felt with Dev. "Bridget, even though he is really . . . interesting, I can't right now."

"Come on, isn't it so much hotter being with a guy that your mom thinks is wrong for you? I say go for it. Use him as a distraction if you can. Being with him might give you a different perspective."

Winnie had no idea what kind of perspective Bridget expected her to get from dating someone else who hadn't even made a move on her . . . sort of.

"I hate to cut off your weird matchmaking dreams, but I need to drown myself in a Vyjayanthimala movie," she said. "Since you aren't coming to the film screening, see you tomorrow in school?"

"Yeah, sorry I can't be there," Bridget said. "If I don't see you before film club, I want a text play-by-play on your meeting with our new Wil Wheaton wannabe faculty advisor," she said.

"Deal."

Winnie knew she was dreaming when she opened her eyes and the air around her lay warm and heavy on her skin. She stood in a gym. A vintage spray-painted Volkswagen was parked in the corner, and a lower level framed by large windows was converted into a dance floor. A lofted second story faced the gym.

Winnie felt another breeze between her legs and looked down. "Gah!" she shrieked, and wrapped her arms around herself. She was half-naked in a pair of Lycra booty shorts and a matching sports bra. Her feet, encased in white sneakers, were the most modestly covered part of her body.

Shah Rukh Khan strolled into the room. His chest was covered in blue Lycra, and the fabric gleamed as he moved closer and tossed her a sweatshirt. She immediately put it on over her tiny outfit.

"Holy crap! Now I know how Karisma Kapoor felt in Dil To Pagal Hai in this outfit."

Shah Rukh Khan grinned. "Times have changed. Actresses are forced to wear less and less. I still prefer the Indian clothes, but we do what we have to in order to please our audience, right?"

"Yeah, I guess. I've never been a fan of the naked look," she said. Winnie hesitated before heading over to the drum set. She sat behind it and tapped one of the cymbals until it hummed with a sweet ring.

"You know," she said, "things would be so much easier if my life was like a Bollywood movie. I'd be my own hero and get my happily-ever-after. But instead I'm pretty sure the prophecy won't come true before my eighteenth birthday, like it's supposed to, and the only time I ever dated someone who could match the prophecy, I don't want him anymore."

Shah Rukh Khan bounced a basketball, then launched it into the air. It made a swooshing sound through the net hanging from one of the gym's beams.

He tsked and said, "That sounds like you've given up. Are you going to go home and watch my movies now?"

She shrugged. "Probably. What else is there to do?"

"Think about the big picture." Shah Rukh Khan tossed her the ball. "You may not believe in it, but you really do have destiny on your side."

Winnie was surprised at the feel of the basketball in her hands. She traced a solid black line before she tossed it back to him. "You're supposed to agree with me. You're from my subconscious."

Shah Rukh Khan dropped the ball and kicked it to the side. He started walking backward toward the dark hallway at the end of the gym. "And isn't it strange that even your subconscious thinks you're interfering with destiny by using free choice as a weapon?"

"What? So not true!" she yelled after him.

"All I'm saying is that if you really desire something from the heart, Winnie, then the whole universe will work with you to get you that. Destiny is showing you the way, and you just have to listen to it. Until next time!"

Winnie watched as he disappeared into a cloud of gray smoke. "Your advice is getting worse with your age, but at least your acting isn't." She picked up the basketball, which had rolled to her feet, and tossed it toward the hoop, enjoying the satisfying sound of the swish as she made nothing but net.

Winnie woke as quickly as she had the last time she dreamed of Shah Rukh Khan. She rubbed the sleep from her eyes, and with images of the actor still circling in her mind, she crawled to the edge of the bed so she could pick up her laptop off the floor. She opened her electronic movie library and scrolled until she saw *Dil To Pagal Hai*. She hadn't watched that movie since she was with Raj. It had so many parallels to the prophecy that Pandit Ohmi had given her. Maybe watching Shah Rukh Khan on-screen could help her come to terms with potentially giving Raj a second chance.

As the first song-and-dance number played, Winnie tried to muster up as much positivity as possible, but she couldn't stop thinking that if destiny was on her side, it couldn't produce Raj as her soul mate. Destiny would have to come up with another solution to her prophecy.

8

AAINA / MIRROR
★★★★☆

It's important to remember that a villain is always the hero in their own movie. They may think they're doing the right thing, but doesn't mean they're right.

"Winnie, did you hear?"

"Man, dude has some moves for trying to win you back."

"Isn't Gurinder one of your favorites?"

"Do you think he did this for you?"

She barely made it to lunch before she had to shut herself in one of the dance studios and go through a quick yoga deep-breathing routine. Mixed with her sleep deprivation, everyone's radiating love for Raj weighed on her heart harder than the breakup itself had. On top of that, she had no idea what Mr. Reece was going to say in their meeting after school now that Raj had proved himself to be so valuable to the film festival.

Her phone buzzed as she reached the auditorium after final bell.

DEV: I met some people when I was working on a sizzle reel about huffing. Rough guys. They said they can hide the body where no one will find it.

She grinned at the message. Even though she hadn't seen him all day, he'd been sending her random images from horror films with Raj's face photoshopped into them.

WINNIE: Thanks, but your phone is potential evidence. We have to keep him alive now. Better take out someone else.
DEV: A Star Trek faculty advisor maybe?
WINNIE: Haha, will let you know how this goes.
DEV: Good luck.

Winnie turned off her phone before stepping into the auditorium and almost running into Jenny Dickens. Jenny looked up; her eyes, lined in neon green, widened.

"What are you doing here?" she said. She looked over her shoulder at Raj, who sat at the edge of the stage.

"Mr. Reece asked me to come."

Her shoulders relaxed a little. "Oh. That's right. I know you want to be the most important person in this film club, but those days are over now that Raj has me to help him. Trying to win him back won't accomplish anything."

"*Excuse* me?"

"You heard me," she said, moving her head like a bobble

doll. "I know everyone is saying you guys should make up since you're the golden couple, but that will *never* happen. He's doing things for himself now and people are giving him the attention he deserves. You won't get him back just because you want to take credit for his work now more than ever. Not while I'm here."

Winnie's eyes narrowed. She stepped forward until she was nose to nose with Jenny. "For someone who's known Raj for a fraction of the time I have, you're pretty cocky, Jenny. Just remember—I'll always have history with the club, with the festival, and especially with my ex-boyfriend."

She smiled when Jenny backed up.

"Whatever. I know you're trying to take him from me, but stay away from Raj, Winnie the Pooh. He's mine now."

"Oh, so clever," Winnie said. Jenny gave her a wide berth and left the auditorium.

Winnie strode down the aisle to where Raj was waiting.

"What did you say to her?" he asked.

"She was catty. She hissed and I roared." She curled her fingers to imitate claws and meowed. "Your new girlfriend has a mean streak."

He grunted. "She's not . . . whatever. Jenny is protective. It's overwhelming sometimes."

"Oh yeah? Well, you dated a super freak like me, so I'm sure you'll work it out with her."

He looked down at his phone. "I don't want to."

"What?"

"Winnie, I told you that I want us to have another shot. That's why I wanted you to keep the bracelet."

"Oh no you don't. I'm giving that back to you."

"No. It's yours. You'll see once I deal with Jenny. I need to figure out how to tell her straight because right now she doesn't understand that I want to end things. I made a mistake." He rubbed his hands over his face. "She's the one who took my phone and posted all those stupid things online about us. She and I will never have what you and I have."

"Raj . . ."

"I begged my dad to get me in touch with Gurinder Chadha's people for you, because I wanted to show you I was serious."

"Don't," she whispered.

"It's the truth. You know it."

"But we can't be the couple we were, and I don't think we should try," Winnie said.

"Then I'll have to work on changing your mind. But we can drop it for now."

"It's not going to happen—"

"Remember when we went to that Bollywood music festival up in Parsippany last year?"

She couldn't help but smile at the memory, even though she knew he was trying to change the subject. With a sigh, she said, "Our laptops wouldn't stream, and the only movie we had on us to watch in the hotel room was—"

"Bend It Like Beckham. You said you'd love to learn from Gurinder Chadha if you had the chance. Maybe you'll get some time to talk to her now. You're better at schmoozing than I am."

The sound of the side door creaking open interrupted them, and Mr. Reece strolled in. He wore a Hulk T-shirt under a tweed jacket.

"Hello, you two," he said. He held up a hand to Raj as he approached. "I'm so proud of you, Raj. You've really done a great job. This film festival is going to be fantastic."

Winnie's nerves crested like a tidal wave. "Mr. Reece? Why am I here?"

He looked over at her, blinking, his mouth setting in a thin line. "Winnie, as you know—as you both know—it's not school policy to allow the same person to hold multiple positions in an organization. Your previous faculty advisor let both of you share the responsibilities, because you've worked so well together, but let's try not to violate school rules. That's why I'm splitting responsibilities, to prevent any administration issues."

Winnie had known that Mr. Reece would do something like this, but her stomach still churned when he confirmed the one thing she was afraid would happen.

"Raj has done a bang-up job with the film festival—"

"After I set up everything last year," she interjected. "No offense, Raj."

"None taken."

"Yes, but he's been innovative and worked very hard to get a guest judge who can really make this festival a success," Mr. Reece responded. "The school will get a lot of publicity."

"Winnie is better at logistics than I am," Raj said. Winnie shot Raj a grateful look.

"I'm aware of her strengths, Raj, but that doesn't mean it's okay to go against procedure. Because of your work, Raj, you'll be the sole point of contact and lead on the film festival. Winnie, you'll remain the president of the film club. I heard there was a great turnout at yesterday's film screening, by the community as well as the student body. It's best if you focus on that."

Winnie couldn't avoid sounding shrill. "You do realize I need this on my transcript, right? The film festival is the only thing that can really make my application shine."

"I'm sorry, Winnie, but rules are rules. You'll figure out some other way to shine. And from what I understand, this might help prevent any awkwardness between you two."

"There isn't any awkwardness! Raj?"

To his credit, he gave Mr. Reece a winning smile. "Nope, we're good. In fact, I need Winnie to be my co-captain. I'll have other stuff that I need to do, so it would be great if she helped."

"Don't worry, you'll have committees to shoulder some of the grunt work," Mr. Reece said. "But you can't share a title with her. Unless you don't want to be a part of the leadership team at all. That means your college application will suffer, too, right?"

Raj hung his head, and Winnie felt her last line of hope snap. She tried to keep the panic from her voice so she didn't sound like Reese Witherspoon in *Election*.

"Mr. Reece, I worked so hard for this. I know you haven't been a faculty advisor for film club before, but you have to understand—"

"No, *you* have to understand," he interjected. "It's my job to follow the rules."

The burning in her chest was painful, so she took a moment before responding. "What would it take for you to make an exception? There has to be a way to make an exception."

"An exception," Mr. Reece said with a sigh. "Okay, there may possibly be room for an exception. According to the rules, a faculty advisor can make an exception to the way school clubs operate based on an extraordinary contribution by an individual student or group of students. If you can demonstrate your leadership capabilities like Raj has, then maybe we'll talk."

"But Ms. Jackson—"

"Ms. Jackson is not your advisor anymore. I run things differently." He looked at his watch. "I'll be back in a few minutes for the meeting. I have a couple calls to make. I'm sorry I don't have better news for you, Winnie. Raj, looking forward to seeing what else you do with the festival."

When he left the auditorium, Winnie groaned.

"I'm sorry, too," Raj said quietly.

"Did you know about this? That he was really going to enforce that stupid school rule?"

"No, but after his email I figured he might mess things up. He's always been crazy about following school rules. I'll talk to him. I wanted to do something special for you. I didn't expect it to make things worse."

"Well, at least he's right about one thing. No awkwardness, since we won't have to work together."

He hopped off the stage. "Don't count on it. I told you, I'm not giving up. I'm the guy your prophecy says is the love of your life. Maybe if I help you with Mr. Reece, you'll see that, too. I'll let you know what I come up with so we can figure this out like we always do. Together. I'll be back. I have to check with my academic advisor on whether or not he sent my transcripts. I'll see you in a few for the meeting."

When she was alone with the sound of the humming air echoing in the empty auditorium, she lay down on the center of the stage. Not only had she been dumped by her longtime childhood friend/boyfriend, but Mr. Reece had dumped her, too.

She looked up into the tangles of wires and lighting equipment in the rafters and pressed a palm to her stomach. It was over. She should give up and apply to be a theater major at the local college. She'd live in her parents' basement for the rest of her life and never see Cannes or study with film theorists like she always wanted, but hey, her parents were awesome. They would still love her even if she was a dead-beat loser.

Winnie heard the doors open again, and muffled voices. She closed her eyes as the footsteps got closer and she felt two people approach her.

"Is she dead?" said a familiar voice.

"No, she's wallowing."

Bridget and Dev lay down, sandwiching Winnie between them. She smelled the rich, musky cologne that clung to Dev on one side, and Bridget's flirty perfume on the other.

"Things just got so bad," Winnie said, and lifted her hands to cover her face.

"So the meeting sucked?" Bridget said.

"Mr. Reece took away my title as film-festival chair. It's against school rules."

They both groaned.

"What are you going to do?" Bridget said.

"Live with my parents for the rest of my life and be a film-buff loser."

"You know what?" Dev said. "This reminds me of one of the few Bollywood movies I've watched in my life. The heroine runs away from home to be with this dude, but she finds someone else on her journey to get there. This other guy is also running away from home. The girl realizes that what she's wanted all along is not for her anymore. There's a lot of songs and they meet in a train. The heroine is as talkative as you."

"I don't think my life story is like *Jab We Met* in this situation."

Winnie's face was so close to Dev's, and his calm and steady gaze helped her focus. A part of her couldn't help but be grateful that things were spiraling out of control. If they hadn't, then she never would have reconnected with Dev.

"I think you have time before the festival to get your title back," Bridget said cheerfully. "When is it again?"

"January fourth," Winnie and Dev said in unison.

Bridget jerked up to a sitting position. "January fourth? Don't you think it's a little strange that you have to find a solution for the film festival with Raj on your birthday? Isn't that your prophecy—ouch!"

Winnie had probably pinched her best friend's thigh hard enough to bruise, but that was the only way to get Bridget to shut up. "There is *nothing* odd about that date. Other than it's going to be here before I know it and I'm screwed."

"So what are you going to do?" Dev asked.

"I wish I knew."

Winnie was beginning to expect the dreams now. She stood on what looked like an empty 1970s Bollywood movie set. Round tables with white tablecloths sat in front of a blue gazebo covered in twinkle lights. She brushed her fingertips against the aqua fabric of her salwar kameez. Long jhumkas hung from her ears, and her anklets chimed when she walked. Man, she wished she could pull the same look off at school.

Shah Rukh Khan wore powder-blue bell-bottoms and sported muttonchops this time. He sat at a piano, playing a familiar song. Winnie approached him and leaned on the piano.

"So I told my dad I'm no longer the film-festival chair."

Shah Rukh Khan continued to play, but he nodded.

"And I know that Raj said he was doing all of this guest-judge business for me, but he screwed my college application in the process. And on top of everything, I'm kinda getting a thing for Dev. It's too soon, though, right? Am I a horrible person for wanting to be with someone else after dating the same guy for years?"

"Only you can answer that question, Winnie," he replied.

"Well, I feel horrible. It's just that, well, Raj and I have known each other for forever. Even though he didn't wait long to date Jenny, I feel like I should wait because I have this prophecy that I'm still not sure about. Also, waiting will give me time to focus on proving myself to Mr. Reece. Whether Pandit Ohmi's prediction about soul mates is true or false, I don't know. But I do know that film is definitely my future."

"Do you think that concentrating on your future is a way for you to avoid your destiny?" Shah Rukh Khan asked.

"I don't know," Winnie said. She closed her eyes, and then had to pry them back open when her false lashes stuck together. "I'm thinking that I need to come to terms with

*destiny being something that I can actually control. It's not
magical and it's not something that can be predicted, no matter what my parents and grandmother and Pandit Ohmi say."*

Shah Rukh Khan gave his iconic wavering laugh.

"What, you don't think that's a good idea?" she said.

"I think that's a foolish idea."

*"Well, I don't. Focus on school; then, after I graduate,
look for a good guy. I'll have to avoid Dev. Avoid Dev and
Raj, I mean."*

*Shah Rukh Khan stood; his fingers slipped from the keys.
He adjusted his cuff links and walked off the set until he was
only a shadow in the darkness.*

*"You're still thinking you can control your future and
you've reached the end of your story, when in fact there
is still much of the movie left to see, my friend." His voice
echoed as he faded.*

*"You need to stop quoting your cheesy movies, Khan!"
she called out. "Oh, and Deepika Padukone totally stole this
movie from you!"*

Winnie jerked awake. She grabbed a half-finished bottle of
warm iced tea off the floor and chugged it.

"Well, that was completely useless," she said in the dark
when her heartbeat slowed.

She powered up her laptop and scrolled through her

video library until she found *Om Shanti Om.* She played the movie from the moment Shah Rukh Khan sat at the piano in the gazebo. She didn't know why she continued to dream about one of her favorite actors, but she was sure that if she played his films, she'd understand what he was trying to tell her. There was no other way to decipher her conversations with him. In the process she'd hopefully get some direction about what she should do.

9

BOMBAY
★★★★☆

This movie is the reason I love Bollywood films. There is a scene where the guy and girl connect. It's quiet, it's quick, but you just know that these two are meant for each other, and they'll fight for their love until the very end.

Winnie carefully lined up film strips in the splicing machine and glued the cut ends together. The sound of the machine, metal rotating against metal, was like music to her ears.

She examined the lead. "Perfect."

"Always so humble."

Henry leaned against the doorway of the projection room. His black eyeliner and matching nail polish contrasted with his tuxedo shoes and Iron Man T-shirt.

"Since I am a hundred percent positive I got this film strip set up right, then why shouldn't I be proud of my awesomeness?"

Henry laughed and pushed off the jamb to come closer.

"You almost done?"

"Yup," she said as she began loading up the platters with film that would then snake through the machine. "What's up?"

"Just wanted to know what your plans are tonight."

"I have to email invites for the next film-club screening, write a movie review for my blog, and edit my college essay. That's about it. Did you have anything in mind?"

"There is a carnival right outside of town. Me and Dev are thinking of going. Want to come?"

She bumped into the prep table next to her, and a stack of empty reels clattered to the concrete floor. "Crap."

Henry crouched down to pick up the reels with her. When they were eye to eye, Henry said, "Winnie, you know I don't notice stuff unless it has to do with processors and film, but even I can tell that you've been avoiding Dev."

"*What?*"

"Seriously. Get a grip, dude. Last Sunday you wouldn't sit next to me and Bridget because Dev was there."

"I had to talk to the marketing committee for the festival! We had to start working on the theme for promo."

"Uh-huh," he said. "And you've worked here three times this week while Dev was on shift with me and you run up here the minute you walk in the door."

"I'm *working.*"

"From those of us who know that Raj is a selfish douche who cheated on you, it's time you move on and give Dev a chance. You guys look, I don't know, *good* together."

She stood, putting the reels back on the table. "There is this Bollywood movie called *Mujhse Dosti Karoge.*"

"Say what?"

"That's the title. It's a line that's repeated in the movie and translates as 'will you be my friend?' Classic love triangle. Guy and girl write letters to each other. Guy comes to India to visit girl, but thinks girl is the hot best friend. Mistaken identity ensues."

Henry shoved his hands in his pockets. "Keep going."

"In the story, the hero gives the heroine a silver bracelet so that his mother would know he chose a bride. Except he has to marry someone else before the truth comes out about who he really wants to be with."

"Okay, now you've lost me."

"All I'm saying is that my truth hasn't come out yet. I'm waiting for the right guy to give me my silver bracelet. Also, I just realized there are way too many Bollywood movies with silver bracelets as a symbol of love."

"Does this mean you can't come hang out with us tonight because you don't want to be friends with Dev? If you want to have a buffer, you can bring . . . uh, Bridget. If she wants to come, I mean. It's not that—I mean . . . Whatever."

"Seriously, Henry?" she said with a laugh. "How long have you been jonesing for Bridget? You've known her for years."

"Damn it," he hissed, turning a darker red than he already had. "She's so perfect, Winnie. And don't tell her! Don't say anything. In fact, forget I mentioned it. It's just this last summer we talked and—no. Never mind."

"Oh no, now we're both *definitely* coming tonight. You just gave me the perfect reason to show up. I'll confront Dev if you confront Bridget. Let me clean up in here and grab my clutch from the office, and I'll meet you guys downstairs."

"Great," Henry murmured.

WINNIE: We're getting food. BTW Henry is so into you.

BRIDGET: WHAT??????!!!!!!!!!????????!!!!!!

WINNIE: It's true. He told me not to tell you so don't say anything.

BRIDGET: OMFGGGG! I'm not coming now!!!!!

WINNIE: Where are u??

BRIDGET: In the parking lot.

WINNIE: Shut up and get in here. Henry's a good guy. Might as well see if u like him too?

BRIDGET: I hate you.

"Bridget will be here in a minute," Winnie said to Henry as she tucked her phone in her clutch. She hoped it really was a minute. She didn't know how much longer she could hide the fact that she was staring at Dev in his fitted shirt as he ordered ice cream at the stall across the walking path.

"Did you tell her? About . . . you know, before?"

"Of course not," she lied. She diverted the conversation to school and work until Dev rejoined them.

"I didn't know what you wanted, so I ordered what I get," he said as he held out a paper cup.

She poked at the ice cream and gasped. "Vanilla bean and Kit Kats?" She dug in until she felt candy, and spooned some into her mouth. The familiar taste had her moaning.

"This is my favorite! I get this every time I go to Robert's Sweets. How'd you know?"

"I guessed. It must be destiny."

She choked and started coughing. Henry reached over and pounded her on the back.

"What are you doing to my best friend?" Bridget asked as she stepped up to them.

"Uh . . . sorry."

"No, it's fine," Winnie said with a wheeze. "Hey, Bridge, Dev got me Kit Kats and vanilla. Did you tell him?"

"Why would I tell him your favorite?"

"She didn't tell me," Dev interjected. "That's my favorite, too. Like I said, I ordered two of the same."

"See, Winnie? It's his favorite. What a coincidence."

Before Winnie could comment, Dev was talking to Bridget. "Henry was telling me that he wants to see if he can win a goldfish at that dunking game."

Bridget's face lit up. "Ooh, can I come?"

"Uh . . . yeah."

"You two have fun," Dev said. "See ya." He curled his

long fingers around Winnie's bicep and pulled her in the opposite direction from where Bridget and Henry had to go.

"Hey!"

"This is their chance to be alone," he said. "Don't you want to see if Bridget and Henry can hit it off?"

Dev was right, which was the only reason she went along with it. They began walking through the stalls and carnival games at a leisurely pace, enjoying their ice cream and the brightly colored signs and sounds. A mother pushing a double stroller tried to squeeze around them, and Dev moved closer to Winnie to get out of the way.

"Want to talk about the festival?" Dev asked.

"We don't have to. Honestly, I'm kind of exhausted with the topic. I never thought I could be, but it's the truth. Even though I don't have the title, I'm trying to show that I'm a leader and I'm doing a lot of the work."

"And you're working at the theater."

"Yes. And trying to avoid early-onset senioritis with my classes."

Dev laughed, and the sound was like Christmas and Diwali rolled into one. "What do you want to talk about if not the festival, work, and school?"

"You choose."

"Okay. Did you start your college applications yet?"

"That's something else I'm working on," Winnie said. "The essays for my NYU application are killing my soul."

"Are you trying for the film studies program?"

"Of course."

He let out a low whistle. "Good luck."

"That's nice," she said with a smile.

"What is?"

"That you know how hard it is to get into NYU. That you understand how hard the essays are to write."

He smiled and reached over to tug a lock of her hair. "Well, I am a movie person, too. And I know that you'll knock those essays out of the park. Even if you aren't film-festival chair anymore, I'm sure you'll do something else that's even better for your application."

"Yo, Dev!" someone yelled.

They turned to see Jai Patel, a junior on the school's South Asian dance team, heading toward them. His date followed in the shortest skirt Winnie had ever seen. She stumbled once on her pencil-thin heels.

"Hey, fancy seeing you here," Winnie said when they stood arm's length apart.

"You guys are here together?" Jai asked.

"Yes."

"No," Winnie said at the same time.

Dev raised an eyebrow at her.

"We're not here *together* together," Winnie said. "We're here at the same time."

When the guys shared a look that she couldn't understand, she turned to Indian Barbie. "Hey, I'm Winnie."

"Hi. Tara."

"Tara goes to Rutgers High," Jai said. "She's on the South Asian dance team there."

"Cool. You guys have an awesome team."

"We do," she replied, before she looked down at her phone.

Jai rolled his eyes. "Hey, the film-club screenings are packed. Awesome mix of movie choices, Winnie. But you know me. I'm psyched about the fund-raiser dance in a few weeks."

"You and the dance team going to show everyone up?" Winnie said with a grin.

"You know it. We'll talk in school. I gotta drop Tara home."

"Yup, see ya later."

Winnie waited until Jai and his date were out of earshot before she said, "I hope he didn't get the wrong impression about us."

"I hope he did," Dev said with a grin.

She elbowed him in the ribs and felt tingly from the contact. "Hey, I want to do the Ferris wheel. You in?"

"No."

"What? Come on!"

"Nope. No way. Kabhi nahin."

When she batted her eyelashes at him and gave him her most innocent smile, he said, "Ugh. Fine."

They started toward the ride. Dev took Winnie's half-melted ice cream, stacked it with his empty cup, and started eating.

"Hey!"

"If you're making me do the Ferris wheel, I'm eating your ice cream."

"I don't get that, but okay."

They maneuvered through the crowds until they reached the end of the line. Dev tossed the empty cups into a nearby trash can and looked up at the giant wheel.

"That's . . . high."

"Yup, and I heard that this one goes around almost a dozen times per ride so we get more time at the top."

"Great . . . just great." He bounced on his heels, and as they got closer to the front, Winnie noticed that Dev's fidgeting worsened.

"You don't like heights," she mused.

"Nope."

"I would've never guessed."

"I hide it well."

"You don't have to go. I can do this by myself."

"That would mean I'm a terrible date."

"Dev, we aren't on a date."

"Next!"

Winnie moved across the steel platform and slipped into the two-seater carriage.

"We can leave—"

"No." Dev's warm fingers laced with hers as they sat pressed together from shoulder to knee. When the lap bar lowered and the carriage jerked forward, Dev's grip on Winnie tightened until her hand ached.

"Dev," she said softly, "I'm sorry. I didn't realize this was that big of a deal for you. There is still time to get off."

"And look like a coward? Bullshit. I committed. I'm following through. But you may need to distract me."

His eyes looked glassy now, and he was swallowing repeatedly.

"What do you want to talk about?"

"Why did you ever date Raj?"

"What?"

"Seriously," he said. "I could tell from day one that you guys had nothing in common other than the movies that you blog about. Why did you date him? When you two were in the bathroom fighting, he mentioned something about him trying to convince you that you were destined. He also gave you a bracelet or something. What's up with that?"

"Yeah, I didn't expect you to want to talk about that."

"You asked."

"I did. Okay. Uh, well. Does your mother have a family astrologer? A pandit?"

He shook his head. "She stopped believing in astrology when my father left us."

Winnie winced. "Ah. Sorry. Well, mine does. We've had the same pandit since before my parents were married. My mom and dad trust him because he gave them two predictions that came true in the strangest way."

"What were the predictions?"

"Decades ago, my mom's mom, my nani, found this really

young priest, Pandit Ohmi, and asked him when the most auspicious time for my mom to get married would be. Pandit Ohmi said that my mother would meet the man of her dreams in an accident, and although she wouldn't get hurt, she'd lose her shoes."

"Are you for real?" he said, his death grip loosening.

"Like Salman Khan's criminal record." She felt the cool breeze against her face as the wheel turned. "And it came true. A few weeks later my mother was in the market with my nani, when the wheel of a small cart broke off and barreled into a bunch of stalls. My father was there, holding a giant watermelon for some reason. He bumped into my mother and dropped the watermelon. It splattered all over her shoes and clothes."

Dev closed his eyes as the first circle completed. "You're joking," he said.

"That's legit what happened. At least that's what they tell me. Dad claims it was love at first sight. Total Bollywood style."

They were halfway through the second turn when she said, "Nani went back to Pandit Ohmi and asked him if the marriage would work. Nani was worried since my mom got really sick when she was a kid and likely couldn't have kids. My dad didn't care, but of course everyone wanted confirmation. The priest said they'd have a child and not to worry. Everyone was so shocked when I was born. Nani and my parents called me a miracle baby, and since then, anything

Pandit Ohmi says, they take at face value. Like the last prediction he made about my family."

"Which is?"

"Pandit Ohmi says my soul mate's name starts with an *R* and he'll buy me a silver bracelet."

His grip on her slackened. "Are you kidding me?"

"Weird, right? I mean, yes, my parents were lucky, but in a way I believed in the prophecy because *they* believe in it."

"Is that why you dated Raj?" he asked.

She shrugged and pulled out of his hold when her palm grew damp. "I saw how great my parents' marriage was, and yeah, I wanted that for myself, too. Raj seemed like the right person. He said all the right things. I liked him."

"This was before or after you and I met in freshman year?"

"You mean before our fleeting friendship?" she said, nudging him in the side with her elbow. "It was during, actually. Raj really started making a case for us to be together around the same time you and I were hanging out. I figured because you two had beef, you didn't want to be friends with me, either, which is why you stopped talking to me."

"That's not true."

"Oh yeah?" Her mouth was dry, but she couldn't stop herself from asking the question. "Then what happened between us?"

"It kind of sucks being with a girl you like when she's dating someone else," Dev said.

Winnie's heart thudded wildly. "You never said anything."

"I never got the chance."

The carriage jerked, and Dev gripped the front of the car. "What's happening?"

They had reached the top again, but since they stopped this time, Winnie was able to admire the view. She could see for miles in either direction. The full moon brightened the sky, and she could see twinkling lights from downtown Princeton in the distance.

Dev, on the other hand, looked like he was going to throw himself off the top. Before she could stop him, he peeked over the edge, and swore expressively.

"Hey!" She grabbed his face. He jerked before their eyes met. The tension holding his body rigid began to loosen.

Click.

Maybe it was Dev, or maybe it was the feeling of weight-lessness as they rocked in the air, the cool breeze gently circling them, and the sounds of the carnival below. Her thoughts scrambled as his gaze dropped to her mouth.

Her eyes drifted shut, and she bridged the distance between them, touching her lips to his.

In that brilliant and sparkling moment, Winnie realized that no Bollywood romance could have ever prepared her for Dev Khanna.

10

CHENNAI EXPRESS
★★★★☆

Conflict resolution comes from two sources in mainstream Bollywood:
deus ex machine, i.e., the gods, and when a friend makes an offhand
comment. I mean, it's cool and all when a god intervenes, but no one
knows more than me the importance of friends in times of crisis.

RAJ: Is it true?

WINNIE: Is what true?

RAJ: You and Dev Khanna. Are you guys hooking up?

WINNIE: WHAT? Where did you hear that?

RAJ: Some of my friends saw you making out at the
carnival.

WINNIE: . . .

**WINNIE: It wasn't making out. We kissed. And why do
you care? You have a new girlfriend, Raj.**

RAJ: Do you like him?

WINNIE: Not even gonna answer that one.

RAJ: Jenny and I broke up for good.

WINNIE: PLEASE don't tell me it's because of me.

RAJ: It's FOR you. Dev tried to hit on you when we were fresh. Not gonna let him win this time either.

WINNIE: I have no idea what you're talking about.

How could Winnie's perspective have changed with one stupid kiss? One stupid, brain-melting, mouth-numbing kiss? She left her phone on top of her bag and lay flat on her back in the empty studio she'd taken over after school. Bridget sat at her hip. They were surrounded by the color-coded index cards that Winnie used to brainstorm for her blog reviews. For some reason, that didn't matter now. None of it did.

"Bridget, what do I do? Seriously, this wasn't supposed to happen. When we got off the ride, we didn't talk *at all*. It was so awkward. We found you guys, and then we left. He didn't even say goodbye to me. Why would he kiss me and then not say goodbye?"

"Technically, you kissed him first."

"He hasn't texted me, either. Why won't he text?"

"And say what? 'Thanks for sucking face while I was losing it on a Ferris wheel. Super sexy of you.' The guy has some pride. Ooh, what if the bracelet is keeping him away? Like a bad-luck charm. I can't believe you didn't tell me that you still had it."

"I wasn't ready to get rid of it when I was burying Raj's movies. Now Raj doesn't want it back. Bracelet aside, Dev could've texted *something*. My phone isn't even on silent anymore, in case he does send me a message."

"That's a big risk for you. Especially with Raj blowing up your cell."

Winnie groaned and covered her face with her hands. "You know that old movie I once told you about, the one from the eighties where the hero and heroine were like forbidden lovers? One of Salman Khan's earliest films."

Bridget rolled onto her stomach. She pulled a lock of hair over her shoulder and started braiding it. "I think you told me about it, but oh, wait, every Bollywood movie that you love and share with me has a forbidden love story."

"Completely untrue. But this one does. Anyway, the heroine tries to communicate with the hero, Salman Khan, by tying her letter to the neck of a pigeon."

"Oh, I do remember!" Bridget said. "The subtitles were so hysterical. The chorus was literally translated as 'pigeon, go, go, go, pigeon, go, go, go'!"

"My point isn't about the pigeon. It's that the hero and heroine had so much faith in this stupid bird to get their message to each other. Meanwhile I can't trust the world's most reliable and fastest wireless network with one stupid text."

Her phone beeped again, and she snatched it up. When she saw Raj's name, she sighed.

"Raj again," she said. "I can't believe he and Jenny are over."

"Focus on the thousand other things you have to worry about. Forget about Dev's kiss and Raj's breakup."

"How would you do it?"

Bridget shrugged. "I wouldn't. It's an impossible idea. I just figured saying it would make you feel better."

Winnie smiled and gave up trying to pry advice out of her best friend. Instead she asked, "How's Henry?"

"You know that eighties movie where they fell in love after knowing each other forever?"

"Ha ha. Very funny. Make fun of me all you want for talking about Bollywood movies like that, but seriously, it's the only way I know how to dissect problems."

"I know. You're strange, but I love ya anyway. Really, Henry is . . . interesting. We'll see what happens. We're seniors, so I don't know where we're going at the end of the school year. What I do know is that he's not what I expected, especially since I've known him, like, forever. He's going to meet us at the homecoming game on Friday."

"Awesome," she said. Even though the Princeton Academy for the Arts and Sciences didn't have a football team, the band played at halftime for other schools. "Can we leave after the third period? Is that what it's called?"

"No, we cannot, and it's called a quarter. I think."

"You suck," Winnie said. She picked up a hot pink card and passed it to her best friend. It had "*Viceroy's House* by Gurinder Chadha" written on the front.

"This reminds me. Henry was wondering if Gurinder Chadha would be interested in a Q&A with students as well as judging."

"A Q&A?"

"Yeah. That might be fun, right?"

"Gurinder Chadha answering questions from students. Wait, if she answers questions . . . I think you're onto something." Her mind raced. "Bridget, you know how every year we have to use the Princeton University faculty as our judges so we can use their auditorium for free? Well, what if we can convince the Princeton faculty that Gurinder Chadha would like to have a master class with them?"

"A master what?"

"A master class. Like filmmaking life lessons learned from a master. Princeton's faculty and their students can participate. It's leveling up the Q&A idea. Maybe the university will accept that instead of judging our festival. That way we don't have to worry about paying for the auditorium."

"I think it could work, but will Gurinder say yes?"

Winnie stood up, her hands filled with notes. "Hopefully, but first I have to get Mr. Reece to say it's okay. This is the leadership thing he was talking about, right? Maybe this will work in helping me take over the festival again."

"I am going to take a nap while you go do that. Good luck!"

Winnie hoped she could still catch Mr. Reece at his office before he left for the day. She was halfway down the hall when she heard her name.

"Wait up!" Dev yelled.

She watched him, all long legs and lean torso. His hair

ruffled with each movement, and she sighed when he pushed it back with a careless brush of his fingers.

And then she remembered they hadn't talked since their kiss.

"Hi," he said when he reached her side.

"Hi."

They stared at each other in silence.

"So," Winnie said. "Are you heading home?"

"No, to the facilities office first. They still haven't fixed my stupid locker."

"At this point, everyone in your hall knows it's broken."

"Very true. Uh, I didn't get a chance to catch up with you after—"

"Yeah?"

"Are you getting back together with Raj?"

Winnie had to shake her head because she wasn't sure she'd heard him correctly. "That's seriously what you want to ask me?"

"I have to admit, it's been on my mind since you told me he fits your prophecy thing."

"Not at all. Raj and I are definitely history. Sorry, I have to go. It was, uh, nice running into you."

She tried to leave, but Dev snagged her hand. She jumped at the warm contact of his palm against hers.

"Are you going to homecoming?" he asked slowly.

"Yes. Why?"

He squeezed and his thumb brushed over her life line.

"Just wanted to make sure you were going to be there. I think it's time for a second date."

She laughed and pulled away. "We haven't been on a first!"

"I bought you your favorite ice cream, we went on a walk, and we took a romantic ride. I think that's a pretty solid first date."

"You ate my ice cream, I dragged you through a crowd, and you wanted to jump off the Ferris wheel."

"I'll make it up to you at homecoming."

Then he did the unthinkable.

He winked at her.

There was no background music or backup dancers. There was no rustling wind or 360-degree camera shot. But with that wink, she felt more with Dev than she'd ever felt with Raj. Winnie liked to think she was strong, independent, and capable. Yet Dev shifted something inside her and her bones melted like goo.

She watched him walk away and then floated the rest of the way to Mr. Reece's office. The wink was still on her mind when she knocked and Mr. Reece called her in. She sank into a chair.

Mr. Reece sat behind his desk, working at his computer. He peered at her over his rectangular frames.

"Yes, Ms. Mehta?"

"Mr. Reece, have you ever heard of the movie *Dilwale Dulhania Le Jayenge*?"

"Oh boy," he muttered, and took off his glasses. "No, I can't say I have."

"It's about this girl who goes on vacation to Europe before her wedding. She meets a guy whose name is, ironically, Raj. He's a jerk to her at first, but they fall in love. When Raj says goodbye at the train station and hands her a cowbell for her to remember their time together, and *boom*! The heroine knows she only wants to be with him. The problem is, she's supposed to marry someone else, and what does she do? Does she follow destiny or run away with Raj?"

"Winnie, what is the point of this story?"

She flung her arms out and tilted her head back. "I think Dev is my Raj because even though he didn't give me a cowbell, he winked! But Raj, the real one, not the one in this movie I'm telling you about, broke up with Jenny, and he's not in my love story at all anymore. Oh, and I think that you can still get the auditorium for free this year if Gurinder Chadha is willing to do a master class with the Princeton faculty."

Mr. Reece chuckled and dropped his head to his desk.

11

DANGAL / WRESTLING
★★★★★

A Bollywood movie, even one about a sport, must have an appropriate amount of drama.

Bridget handed Winnie a pumpkin-spice latte with the name Vinny written on it in black marker.

"Thanks, boo," Winnie said.

A chill in the air whipped through her clothing and iced her skin. She hunched over her cup, hoping to absorb some of the heat. Her hair gave some added protection since she wasn't sporting a braid for once, and Bridget had nagged her into taking the time to flat-iron. She could still have used a sweatshirt, though. Long-sleeve shirts weren't going to cut it.

"Thank Starbucks, *Vinny*. I'm so happy they have a drive-through down the block," Bridget said. "I can't stand the slushy crap they serve here."

Winnie looked down at a really important white line that

she didn't know the name of. She was sitting in a half-full stadium.

"So are you coming to my mom's pooja next weekend?" Winnie asked.

"Considering your mom specially invited me to come and pray for your slutty soul, of course I'll be there."

"My slutty soul could always use your support. Although it wouldn't be slutty if I kept things to myself. Telling my mother that I have a thing for Dev was not one of my better ideas."

"You can say that again," Bridget said. She looked at her phone screen and then scanned the stadium.

"Is Henry on his way?"

"He's walking in now. What about Dev?"

"He texted me a few minutes ago to ask what section we were seated in."

Bridget wrapped an arm around Winnie's shoulder and squeezed. "Are you nervous?"

"Excited. I feel like I should be nervous, though, only because I have no idea what we're doing. Am I rebounding because of my super-long relationship with Raj? It doesn't feel like rebounding, probably because I sort of maybe had a thing for Dev in freshman year, too. Before Raj."

"Then it's probably not rebounding," Bridget said.

"Hey, guys," Henry said as he approached their row. He smiled at Bridget, not even acknowledging Winnie's presence.

"Hi!" Bridget said with a little too much bubbly in her

voice. She scrambled to her feet so she could give him a hug. They stood in the dimming stadium lights, wrapped around each other for a moment, and Winnie felt a slow warmth in her stomach for her best friend.

"Henry," Winnie said after the couple pulled apart. "It's nice to see you outside of work and school."

"Yeah, what up?"

"Did you see Dev up there? He was supposed to be here by now, too."

"Actually, he was right behind me," Henry said.

Someone on the field blew a horn, and Dev dropped down next to her.

He took over the space with his man-smell and confidence. He was so much broader and taller than her that even though they were sitting next to each other, she felt that he was stealing the very air she was breathing. Worse, Dev wore a beanie and a leather jacket.

Holy baby Shah Rukh Khan. No music or backup dancers, but that strange feeling was there again.

"Hey," he said.

"Hi."

He tugged on a lock of her hair. "Pretty. What's that?" he asked, pointing to her cup.

"Oh. Um, a PSL. Why?"

He plucked the cup from Winnie's hand and brought it to his mouth to take a sip.

"Dev!" He put his mouth right over the spout. If she drank

from it now, it would be as if their lips were in the same place and they were kissing again.

"Ugh," he said as he handed the cup back to her. "That's such a girl drink."

"First of all, drinks do not have genders. And second, you ate my ice cream the last time we went out, and I was too distracted to really care then, but this is my latte we're talking about. If you have a thing against the PSL, don't touch mine."

They stared at each other for a moment and then shared a grin.

"Hey, Dev," Bridget said, leaning around Winnie. Her eyes sparkled with mischief. "I didn't think you'd be the type to come to a football game."

"Nope, but I've never done the expected."

"Good point," Bridget said.

Before Winnie could comment, an icy breeze hit her, and she shivered.

"Where's your coat?" Dev asked.

"I was an idiot. Completely forgot it."

After a minute he stood. "I'll be right back."

He was gone before Winnie could respond. Someone on the field blew a horn and everyone started cheering. Cheerleaders waved their pom-poms, and the marching bands played something peppy. The teams began pouring from separate corners of the stadium onto the field. Winnie checked her phone and then braced herself for another gust of wind. She shivered harder this time.

"I'm going to warm up on the main level," she said, poking Bridget in the side. She figured she'd return before Dev got back.

"Do you want me to go with you?" Bridget asked.

"I'm good. Be back in a sec."

Winnie reached the main concourse, crammed with food vendors and people, and instantly felt better out of the wind. After scanning the crowd for Dev, Winnie headed for the restroom to check on her hair when she spotted Raj and Jenny standing off to the side. From the way Raj was looking at everything but Jenny, arms folded, shoulders hunched, he was totally getting eaten alive.

She tried to give them a wide berth as she passed. Dealing with Raj and Jenny while she was on a date was the last thing she wanted to do. She almost managed to sneak by, but Jenny swung around and stopped her.

"You!" she shouted. "You broke us up because you were jealous!"

Winnie winced. Jenny's voice carried in the echo of the concourse level, and some people had already stopped to see where the yelling was coming from.

"Jenny, this isn't her fault," Raj said.

Winnie looked at the bathroom door in the distance and tried to hustle toward it.

"That's right, just ruin this and run away!" Jenny shouted. "You only care about yourself and your stupid movies."

Jenny's words had her skidding to a halt. All plans for making a quick exit vanished. She stormed over until she was standing next to Raj. "You knew Raj and I had been together for years, and you're pointing fingers at *me*? Didn't he tell you we were on a break?"

Jenny's bloodshot eyes widened before cooling. Her tongue licked at her chapped lips. "Everyone knows that if you're on a break, you're broken up."

"Why the hell do people believe that?" Winnie said, arms flailing. "But whatever—we're broken up for real now. I told him that we were over. Your relationship is your business."

"Well, he wants you back, so congratulations. You won." Jenny spun on her heels and stormed off.

Everyone was going to hear about this before school on Monday, Winnie thought.

Raj leaned against the brick wall, scrubbing his hands over his face. He looked so miserable.

Winnie hesitated, and then said, "You okay?"

"You've been avoiding me."

"Probably because you and Jenny obviously have something, and I don't want to get in the middle. I never thought I'd say this, but you should try to work things out."

"I broke things off with Jenny because *you* matter to me. You're still the love of my life. It's not just your prophecy and future at stake; it's mine, too, since I think we're destined here."

"If that's the case, then you wouldn't try to change me. I'm going to NYU. If you really had feelings for me, you'd help me solve this film-festival problem instead of thinking that *I'm* the problem. We're officially over and in the past."

"If what you're saying is true, then you would've gotten rid of my bracelet with my movies. But you kept it."

Her cheeks warmed. "I've been trying to give it back to you for weeks! You're the one being a butthead about it."

He pushed off the wall and stepped closer until they were only inches apart. He looked down at her, and for the first time in all the years she'd known him, he had a cockiness on his face that she'd never seen before.

"You may think I'm doing this because of your horoscope, but I'm actually doing it for me, too. For us. We're good together. I just have to remind you of that."

"Nope. Sorry. Not gonna happen." She turned to leave, but he gripped her arm and pulled her back a step. It felt nothing like Dev's touch.

"I'm fighting for you, Winnie," he said, louder. "Like the heroes in your favorite movies. Which, by the way—I know them all. Does anyone else? No one. Maybe not even Bridget."

Before she could pull away, his hand was ripped off hers, and he grunted as she heard a smacking sound of body meeting cement.

Dev pinned Raj to the wall with his forearm pressed against his neck. He had a sweatshirt draped over one shoulder, and his other hand was pushing against Raj's chest.

"Dev! What are you doing? Let him go," she hissed. Her heart pounded as she watched them press closer, struggling against each other. Raj was a lot thinner and shorter than Dev, but he was able to push him away.

"Touch her again, and I'll do more than put you in a choke hold, asshole," Dev said through clenched teeth.

Raj shoved Dev, and Dev braced himself to do the same.

"Raj, Dev, stop it!" Winnie yelled. This was getting out of hand. "Dev, let's go. Raj, go home."

Dev looked at her, then at Raj. "Stay away from her."

"Screw you, asshole! You've always been jealous of us."

Before Dev could move in again, Winnie pushed them away from each other. "I will seriously hurt you both if you don't stop. I took kickboxing once, and I could do it."

She gripped Dev's arm, intending to lead him to the bleachers. Raj let out a humorless laugh. "Wait a minute. Are you kidding me? The rumors are true! You're actually dating him?"

"We're not *dating*," Winnie said. "Come on." She motioned to Dev.

"Why does it matter to you, dickhead?"

Raj crossed his arms over his chest. "Winnie and I are getting back together."

"No, we aren't."

"Three years and you're still clueless," Dev said to Raj. "And yeah, we *are* dating." He reached for her hand and linked his fingers with hers.

They maneuvered through a swarm of people until finally they reached the archway that led down to their bleacher section. Winnie pulled him to a stop.

"Dev, you can't jump people like that!"

"I thought he was hurting you."

"And what, you think I can't take care of myself? I know him better than you do. Raj may be misguided, but he's not violent." Winnie shivered when the brisk wind rushed up her back.

Dev took the sweatshirt off his shoulder and passed it to her. "Here," he said. "I was going to give you my jacket, but I figured no sense in both of us being cold."

It was soft, and it felt worn in, like it had gone through the wash a few times. She almost brought it to her face and buried her nose in it. She hesitated before slipping it over her head. The sweatshirt smelled like him, and in that moment she knew she was never going to return it. Some of her frustration ebbed.

"Thanks."

"Winnie?"

"Yeah?"

He brushed a strand of hair off her face. "I'm not going to let freshman year happen again, okay?"

"Freshman year?"

Before she could stop him, Dev touched her chin and pressed the softest, quickest kiss against her mouth.

"Wh-what was *that* for?" Winnie asked when she could make coherent sentences again.

"I'm not going to ignore Raj while he tries to make another move."

"He can't. He *won't*. I don't want him to. But, Dev, this is too much, too fast. I just got out of a thing with Raj."

Dev raised an eyebrow. "Are you sure you're over him? Because having destiny on his side is a pretty strong argument."

"I'm spending time with you, not him," she said quietly. "Doesn't that count for something?"

"Yeah. Yeah, it does."

She linked her fingers with his again and led him toward the stadium seats. "Maybe at halftime you can buy me nachos and not eat them."

"And maybe you'll wake up tomorrow hating Bollywood movies."

She laughed. "Okay, okay. I can forgive you for taking my nachos because you tried to defend my honor. I appreciate you fighting Raj, but it's not necessary."

"Your doucheweed ex doesn't know what he's up against. He may have the prophecy on his side, or so he thinks, but so do I."

Winnie stopped halfway down the stairs. The hair rose at the nape of her neck. "What does that mean?"

"Nothing. There are some things I should probably tell you because of this whole prophecy thing you have in your star chart, but you have to trust me when I say that it doesn't matter. After all, you don't believe in the prophecy anymore anyway, right?"

"Uh, yeah, I guess not." When they finally sat down next to Bridget and Henry, Winnie tried her best to watch the game and her friends, but something Dev had said wouldn't stop circling in her mind. What did he have to do with the prophecy?

Like any Bollywood heroine worthy of her role, Winnie spent the rest of the game wondering if the hero she was with had a more tangled backstory than the one who'd gotten away.

12

YAADEIN / MEMORIES

★★☆☆☆

Personally? I don't think all the praying in the world on the part of the father could've saved the heroine and her sisters from looking like idiots.

The most common element in all Bollywood pooja scenes was the number of people in attendance. That was because in real life, poojas could potentially involve a gazillion family members, friends, and distant acquaintances.

Winnie hated all the prep work that went into it. A pooja meant the furniture had to be moved to the front sitting room. Then the living room had to be swept, mopped, and dusted. Every single area rug in the house had to be moved into the living room, vacuumed, and then covered with blankets and sheets for people to comfortably sit on the floor. Lastly, the coffee table had to be pushed against the far wall and then draped in a bright red mesh cloth to display the statues from the small temple upstairs.

The work was grueling, and Winnie had no idea how her

parents did everything so tirelessly. They were old, and they still had more energy than she did. Her excuses about having to do homework and college-application essays fell on deaf ears. She had to help. Her back ached as she finished setting the last of the statues on the coffee table at her father's instruction.

"We are done here," he said, pushing his glasses up the bridge of his nose. He rested his hands on his hips and stretched to the side. "Now all we have to do is get dressed. People will be here soon. See if there is anything else to do before you get changed."

Winnie stifled her groan. "Fine. I'll check with Nani and Ma." She followed the sound of arguing into the kitchen. Her mother and grandmother were standing at the stove, nudging each other over for more space. Her mother was rolling dough while her grandmother made comments about technique. Winnie would've helped if she didn't have a history of setting things on fire. She was useless in the kitchen and her family knew it.

"The puris aren't big enough."

"Muma, they're fine."

"I've seen your fat friends. You need to make them bigger."

"My friends are not all fat, and this is fine."

Nani and Ma had been working for days making dry chole and puris. Huge silver pots sat on the stove with the small chickpeas cooking over a slow heat. The front burners each held a wok filled with oil, which sizzled every time a small, flat, circular piece of dough slid into the hot liquid. After the dough puffed into a bubble, Nani pinched the corner with tongs, flipped it over, then tossed it into the disposable serving tray on the counter next to her.

"Are you guys almost done? I'm starving."

"You cannot eat until after the pooja," her mom said. "It's only a few hours, Winnie. Drink some water."

"We still have to heat the tari aloo and the halwa," Nani said. Just the mention of the potato curry and the sweet dessert made Winnie's mouth water.

"Oh God, Muma," her mother said. "Move! I can do this faster by myself. People will be here soon."

"No, you can't, because the oil is too hot. You'll burn yourself."

"Muma, I'm almost fifty. I've been having my own pooja and making puris for more than twenty years. I can handle the hot oil!"

They continued to work in tandem even as they yelled at each other. Winnie took a bottle of water from the fridge and escaped to her room. She figured they would've said something if they'd needed her.

Winnie grabbed her phone off her bedside table and hopped onto her bed. She was about to check her messages when Raj's face popped up on the screen. She debated letting it go to voice mail, but after four rings she caved.

"What?" she said.

"Still mad?"

"Raj, my personal life is no longer your business."

"I'm sorry. Really. I'm still getting used to us not being together, even if it's only temporary."

"I'm hanging up."

"No, wait," he said. "It's about the film festival. I wanted to let you know that Gurinder approved the master-class idea. She loves it and is willing to work with whatever schedule we set. We just have to let her know in advance."

She vaulted up in bed. "What? For real?"

"Yup. Now you have to convince the Princeton faculty to like it."

"Holy baby—holy crap!" She squealed and bounced on her bed. "Raj! This is awesome. If Mr. Reece sees this as initiative, maybe he'll let us both lead the festival again." Her mind raced as she thought about all the possibilities for the master class and festival.

"Yeah, Reece knows this has been your thing from the get-go, so I think you have a good chance."

"Really? I'm still annoyed about homecoming, but thank you for this. When I didn't hear from you, I thought you were going to just take it over."

"Come on, I'm not that big of a jerk," he said. "I had to wait for the right time. Now you can take credit for all the work you've been putting in on the fund-raiser dance, too."

The fund-raiser. That was another thing Winnie was trying to squeeze into her schedule. "I don't know how to thank you for this."

"You could go out with me. You know. Like old times. Then I could really apologize."

"Nope. Sorry. It's not going to happen."

"It was worth a shot," he said. Voices echoed in the background, and Raj murmured something in response before saying, "I gotta go. I miss you. Let me know if you need any help with talking to the Princeton faculty, but I know you got this."

"Definitely. Thanks again!"

"Bye," he said, and hung up.

Winnie looked over at the bracelet sitting on top of her dresser. One thing was for sure: he was trying to make things work. That didn't mean she had to give him a chance, though. Destiny or not.

She hoped.

Bridget pushed open her bedroom door and flung her arms wide. "Make me Indian beautiful," she said.

"I can definitely do that," Winnie said with a laugh. Thoughts of Raj took a backseat as Winnie grinned at her best friend.

"Dress-up montage!" they yelled.

For the next half hour, Winnie and Bridget tried on most of the clothes in Winnie's closet. Finally Bridget settled on a bright lemon-and-pink salwar kameez, while Winnie chose an outfit her grandmother bought her last Diwali.

"Wow, are you going to add bling to that?" Bridget asked

when Winnie pressed the hanger to her collarbone to check the length.

"Probably some jhumkas. Why, does it need more?" The tunic had a square neckline and fit her to mid-thigh. The balloon pants were pleated in the front and cinched at her ankles. The entire outfit was royal blue with a continuous gold embroidered border, and it came with a sheer lime-green chuni that draped over her shoulder.

Bridget's arm snaked around her waist and squeezed. "No. You're going to look gorg. I'm wondering what Dev will say when he sees you all traditional. After the game, and the way you guys have been staring at each other all week, everyone knows that you're together."

"On Wednesday night, Dev spent his break in the projection room with me. I worked on splicing and we just talked about, I don't know, everything. It was really, really nice."

"And even with college applications, school, your blog, and film club, you're looking happy again, Winnie. That's awesome."

Winnie blushed. "Well, today is going to be challenging and not so happy. I'll be running around with my mom, so if Dev says something to you, let me know." She slipped tiny gold drop earrings into her earlobes, pushed bracelets onto her wrists, french-braided her hair, and tied it with a matching lime-green tie that had gold beadwork along the edges.

She curled tiny strands of hair at her temple to frame her face and helped Bridget do the same.

They stood together in front of the closet's full-length mirror.

"I think you should selfie, Bridge. For Henry."

"He's been texting me. He says he's coming over tomorrow to watch the six-hour *Pride and Prejudice* so I can educate him on BBC miniseries."

Winnie gripped her shoulders. "I want to hear about everything after he leaves."

"Of course. That goes without saying."

They opened the bedroom door when they heard the first ring of the doorbell. After that, the rest of the afternoon was a blur. Winnie said hello to all the aunties, uncles, and kids at the front door. She helped serve water, welcomed the priest, who sat next to the makeshift altar, and then when they had to get started, she settled next to her mom, Nani, and dad at the front. Winnie knew that Bridget would take care of Dev when he showed up.

Poojas were such a pain for her . . . literally. Her foot would fall asleep because she had to sit cross-legged the whole time, and then when she tried to shake her limbs awake, her mother usually shot her a look that could immobilize a crowd in the middle of a Holi celebration at a hundred yards.

This pooja was going to be particularly agonizing because it was for *her*. To her family's credit, they'd let all the guests think it was a Durga pooja for Navratri, the nine-night festival that started the following week, but Winnie's mom had made it clear to her that they were praying for her since she was blatantly disregarding her horoscope and Raj.

Out of the corner of her eye, Winnie saw a flash of black. Dev was in jeans and a button-down shirt, leading a woman to a spot in the corner of the room. The older woman had streaks of white hair at her temples, but her wide, moon-shaped face was bright, young, and cheerful. She wore a pale lavender salwar kameez with a chuni draped over her head. It was a distinctly Punjabi style, much like what Winnie's own mother wore.

Dev's mom, Winnie thought, as the pandit started a series of really long prayers. Winnie had insisted they be invited. She looked over at them one last time and tried to pray her heart out.

Like some of her Hindu friends, she didn't really know the exact words, but she'd developed the ability to move her lips in the rhythm of the prayers so it seemed as if she was saying the right verse even when she had no idea what was actually going on. In the movies, whenever there was a pooja scene, the director would focus in on one of the gods and then on the hero or heroine, who would recite an internal monologue about what he or she wished to accomplish. Winnie closed her eyes and tried to be as sincere as possible as she started her internal monologue.

Hey, Durga Ma, I know this pooja is to thank you for being awesome, and I know that my mom is doing this for me. Even though they're totally weird, please bless my mom and dad for all that they do. Second, thanks for keeping me in the game with this film-festival thing, but can I ask for one teensy thing? I really want Pandit Ohmi's prediction for my big Bollywood romance to go away. I like Dev, and this prophecy is hanging over my head like a swinging ax. I've made up my mind. So if you could help me there, that would be great. Thanks.

Winnie wrapped up her prayer and put on her best pretend face as her family finished up the pooja. She said "swaha" when she was supposed to and threw raw rice into the fire. When her mother and grandmother told her to help pass out the prasad, Winnie tried to maintain her poise, even though she knew Dev was watching her the whole time. The guests were chatting with each other, but there was an odd lull of silence just as her mother said to the priest, "Although we are praying to Durga for Navratri, I want to ask especially for my daughter to find the love that she has been promised in her janampatri. A love that will shower her with more than a silver bracelet."

The room went silent, and Winnie froze, empty tray in hand, as everyone stared at her. She heard snickers and coughs from behind her and knew that the whole room had heard what her mother said. Horoscopes might have been all the rage in Hinduism, but actually admitting to believing in them was embarrassing.

"I need more of this," her grandmother said in Hindi from her spot on the floor. She chugged what looked like water from a bottle. Winnie scanned the room to see that everyone was still staring.

Seriously, Durga Ma? Not. Cool. She continued serving food as if nothing had happened, but she really wanted the pooja to be over already.

Right after she finished handing out the prasad, Winnie headed upstairs. She was going into hiding, and she didn't care if that insulted her family or her parents' guests. There was a small space between her bed and the wall, the perfect spot for curling into the fetal position, and that was where she intended to stay until she had to drag her butt to school on Monday. Did her mother really have to open her mouth in front of the Indian kids that went to her school? Did she have to talk in front of Dev?

Bridget followed her to her room and tried to coax Winnie back, but Winnie refused. When Bridget mentioned Dev, Winnie felt a twinge of guilt for sure, but she still couldn't face him.

A little after Bridget returned downstairs, Winnie heard her bedroom door squeak open, and she hunched her shoulders, hoping that no one would see her.

"Hey," Dev said.

Winnie popped up from her hiding spot. "What are you doing up here? You can't be in my room."

He rolled his eyes and closed the door behind him. "What, because your virtue will be ruined and your family's name will be tarnished if we're alone together? Come on, it's the twenty-first century, Winnie. Besides, both of us are used to people talking about us, right?"

It was her turn to roll her eyes. "Not like this. My mother makes me sound so *desperate*. Ugh, I hate it. Everyone is whispering about how sorry my situation is."

If she hadn't been watching him, she would've missed his jaw clenching and his eyes going cold at her words. "I'm used to people talking about me exactly like this," he said.

Then he glanced at the far wall and did a double take. "Holy shit." He was across the room, reaching for her movies, before she could straighten her chuni.

"This is unreal," he said as he scanned the titles from top to bottom. His voice was low, almost reverential, looking at the size of her collection. "Is this all yours? This is so sick. You have the largest Bollywood collection I've ever seen!"

Winnie was grateful for the distraction as she checked out the room to make sure she didn't have anything embarrassing lying around.

"They're my pride and joy," she said after tucking a discarded bra under her blanket.

He stopped reading the spines when she reached his side.

"Indian clothes look good on you," he said, brushing the edge of her sleeve.

Winnie felt that weird flutter in her stomach. "Thanks. And thanks for coming. I know it's all a little awkward."

He grinned. "My mom doesn't get out as much as she used to, and it was cool to see her excited to get dressed up and all." His fingers skimmed over the titles and landed on a copy of the movie *Dil To Pagal Hai.* He murmured "aha" before pulling the movie off the shelf and holding it up against his chest.

She looked at the cover, and an image of it lying in the dirt flashed in her mind: she'd buried it with Raj's collection. "It's stupid. Can we not talk about it?" She went over to the small bench at the end of her bed to sit down.

Dev tossed the DVD back and forth a couple times before sliding it onto the shelf. "I mean, why wouldn't it be? This dude falls in love with this dancer. She wears a silver bracelet. However, she's supposed to marry someone else. Love triangle ensues."

Dev sat down next to her on the bench, elbows braced on his knees, fingers interlinked.

"That's why you wore the silver bracelet all the time. That was the bracelet Raj gave you," he said. "Winnie, I hate to sound like a broken record, but you have to admit he does seem to meet all of your prophecy requirements. You may not believe in destiny, but that silver bracelet is hard to argue with."

She shook her head. "It's not hard at all."

"Why do you say that?"

"Raj and I grew up together, remember? Our parents talked about it all the time. It was expected that he would buy me the bracelet at some point. He finally gave it to me when we started fighting last year. It was probably a way to try to keep the link between us when we both knew it was falling apart."

"But despite the bracelet, the history, his name, you still asked for a break, because he didn't understand what you wanted to do with your future."

"Pretty much. Do you know why people love Bollywood movies so much? In general, I mean."

"Not for their contribution to the cinematic art, for sure."

She smiled. "There are some amazing movies that defy the Bollywood stereotype, but for the most part, the acting has been criticized as overdramatic, the plotlines sometimes don't make sense, and there are song-and-dance numbers that have no connection to the story setting."

"Then why?"

"People love the movies because of the romance, the emotion, and the passion the characters feel. It's easy to get swept up in the magic as long as you have a flexible suspension of disbelief."

Dev leaned into her arm, and she felt a tingle at the base of her spine from the contact. "That's for sure," he said.

"For me, Pandit Ohmi's prediction means that I'll have

that romance with someone, have that kind of love and passion. But it's predetermined. Like Bollywood movies. My life is set for me. I'm the heroine and this one particular guy is the hero and I have no choice. When Raj first asked me out, I said yes, because I felt like I was making a conscious decision to accept the prophecy. At least that's what I told myself."

"So it was a way to take control of your destiny," Dev said. "And if you stayed with him and you didn't act in your best interest, it would be giving in to your destiny."

"And now I know that if I consciously choose to be with someone because of their name, because of a piece of jewelry that they give me, I'm letting destiny control me, and I can't have that. As much as I want my prophecy to be true, I want it to be true because *I* made it happen."

"Free will. Okay, that makes sense to me."

Dev wrapped an arm around her shoulder and filled her space like he'd been filling her thoughts.

"When I was fourteen, my dad left us," he said. "He'd been cheating on my mom with a coworker, and one day he came home and said that she was pregnant and he didn't want me or my mom anymore. He left everything in the house to us but cleaned out the bank accounts, and then he married this other woman."

The confession was so unexpected that Winnie didn't know how to respond. If one of Winnie's American friends at school had told her the same story, she would have been sympathetic for sure. Dev was an Indian American, though, and because of some archaic cultural traditions, divorce could be considered worse than death. There was a good chance that some people had been cruel. The blunt truth of his life felt like a slap.

"Oh my God, Dev."

"Yeah," he said. "And my parents had what the priest called a 'perfect match.' Their star charts matched over twenty-five points, which is supposed to be excellent. They let others tell them what to do, and it ruined my mother's life. She should've trusted her instincts."

"Dev, I'm so sorry. I don't even know what to say."

Dev reached over to cover her hand with his. "Say that you understand. That you realize predictions about destiny, astrology readings, whatever, can be incredibly misleading. However, if they match what you want for yourself, you won't avoid someone just because destiny and free will are the same. Screw pandits and star charts and prophecies. Sometimes you have to trust yourself and let destiny follow."

"Easy for you to say," she mumbled. "My problem is, how can I know for sure if my prophecy is what I want since it's been crammed down my throat since birth? My mother even mentioned it at the pooja just now."

"Have you tried to go with your gut?"

She looked up at him. "If I had, then maybe you and I would've dated freshman year."

He smiled and pulled her closer. He tilted her head back and then rested his lips against hers. As kisses went, it was pillow soft and cotton-candy sweet. She closed her eyes and leaned into him.

"Go out with me again," he said when they came up for air.

She dropped her head to his shoulder. It felt right, so she said the only thing her filmi soul wanted her to say.

"Okay."

13

★★★☆☆

Regardless of whether a film is a Hollywood or Bollywood production, a shopping montage must always result in the perfect outfit.

852-4655: Why cant u leve Raj ALONE?? Isnt Dev enuf?

WINNIE: I want nothing to do with Raj romantically. We just work together so STOP TEXTING ME.

852-4655: STOP TALKING TO RAJ.

WINNIE: Get over it. I'm blocking you.

Winnie surveyed the chaos around her. A laptop sat on the dark wood coffee table next to a cup of iced chai latte, her cell phone, and a stack of textbooks and notebooks. Pulled up on the computer screen was the final draft of her essay for her application. A v-chat box was open in the right corner. Bridget's face filled the small window, her long hair piled on top of her head in a messy knot. Instead of her usual contacts, she wore large hot-pink frames that dwarfed her face.

"I'm exhausted," Winnie said. Her words were muffled by the royal blue decorative pillows edged with silver mirror embroidery.

"You asked for it," Bridget replied. "Your application is finally finished, though!"

"Yeah, but I'm not submitting it until I know for sure about this film festival."

"Right. All the entries are coming in, apparently. Raj asked you to review them, right? It looks like some good stuff, too."

"I hope so, since we have a guest judge who is also teaching the master class."

"You're about to take on *all* of the work for the festival, aren't you? Raj has been waiting for this moment. I bet you even have the fund-raiser dance on your plate."

Winnie grunted.

"I'm sorry, I don't understand pathetic." Bridget clapped her hands, and the sound was like an alarm blaring through the speakers of her laptop. "Come on! What's up?"

"Nothing. You're right, it is going to be a lot more work if I get to be festival co-chair again. I thought I'd be excited about it, because my college application is going to rock, but there is so much more going on now, you know? Dev, Raj . . . and Jenny is still being all psycho and texting me. I finally blocked her."

"She texted you again? How does she know if you and Raj talk?"

"Because she has spies, Bridget." Winnie leaned close so

that she could peer into the webcam at the top of her laptop monitor. "Jenny has spies *everywhere*."

Bridget snorted. "You're a freak, you know that?"

"I'm losing my mind. Did I mention that I have a calc test on Friday? That's right before I go to work at the theater."

Before Bridget could respond, Winnie's grandmother strolled into the living room holding two glasses filled with a smoothie drink. Her mother walked in behind her with a plate of spicy potato noodles.

"The girl doesn't eat," Nani said as she handed Winnie one of the glasses. "This is good for you. Mango lassi. Drink it."

"Oh, okay. Where did you get the aloo bhujia?" Winnie said, pointing to the plate with her other hand. "I thought Dad ate the rest of the bag. Did you take a trip to Subzi Mandi today?"

"No, we tried the new Patel Brothers grocers that opened next to Neelam Auntie's development."

Her grandmother put on the glasses that were hanging from the collar of her sweatshirt and sat down on the couch. She peered at the screen and scrunched her nose.

"Ai ki hai?" she asked. "What is this?"

Bridget waved, and Winnie made the window wider. "Hi, Nani!" Bridget said. "Hi, Auntie."

Nani leaned closer and started yelling, loud enough for Winnie's ears to ring. "Oh, Bridget! Nice to see you! You come over soon and I feed you, okay? We make Indian food. No spicy for you! Come soon!"

"Nani!" Winnie said, covering her ears. "Bridget and I are both going to go deaf. You don't have to yell at the screen. And why are you talking so weird? She knows that you speak better English than that."

Nani smacked Winnie on the back of the head.

"Ouch!"

She yelped again when her mother smacked her, too.

"What was that for?"

"Disrespect," both women said in unison.

Bridget was laughing on the other end. "What are you two beautiful women up to?"

Sita Mehta got close to the screen and motioned over her shoulder at Winnie. "You know, this one works too hard. We're thinking of taking her out."

"Drink your lassi and eat some bhujia," Nani said. "After that, we're going shopping!"

"I have to get to school early tomorrow, and I have homework and film-club stuff to do."

"You need a mental interruption," her mother said, patting her thigh. "Eat your share of bhujia before your father finishes this, too, and then get ready. We're going to Oak Tree Road."

"Wait, we're going *Indian* shopping?"

Bridget started squealing on the screen. "Can I come, too? Oh my God, I love Oak Tree Road! We can get the anklets you've been promising me."

"Yes, you come, too!" Nani shouted before getting up to go. "See you, Bridget!"

"Ten minutes," Winnie's mother added. "Bridget, if your mother approves, we'll drive, okay?"

"Okay, thanks, Auntie."

Winnie waited until they left the room before she placed her lassi on the coffee table and fell into the cushions and throw pillows again. "Why would you egg them on, Bridget? You know how bad Indian shopping with my mother and grandmother can be. I spend most of the time trying to convince them not to buy out the entire store for me."

"Do you know how lucky you are to have a mom and grandmother who love bling? We're going to have so much fun."

Winnie slammed closed the lid of her computer.

Oak Tree Road in Edison, New Jersey, was one of America's finest Indiatowns. Even on a weeknight, the long two-lane street lined with Indian restaurants and clothing stores was congested with drivers and pedestrians wearing a mix of western and traditional Indian clothes. Although there were a few Indian stores in Princeton and even more in North Brunswick, Winnie's mother still liked to drive the forty-five minutes to Edison so she could get her eyebrows threaded and buy groceries. Today they were skipping the groceries and heading straight for the clothing boutiques.

"Let's go in here," her mother said, pointing to one of the

shops toward the end of the strip. They passed the kebab store with its opened windows and meat cooking on three-foot-long skewers. The rich, pungent smell was mouth-watering.

"Ma," Winnie groaned, pressing a hand to her stomach. "Let's stop here first. The lassi and bhujia weren't enough for dinner."

Her mother kept pulling her along, past a group of elderly women dressed in saris. Bridget trailed behind in her tight jeans, her blond hair waving like a yellow beacon.

"Right now we have to go see some outfits for you." Her mother wrapped an arm around her shoulder and leaned in to press a sloppy kiss against her cheek. "This is all for you, beta. Don't be rude, otherwise your grandmother is going to throw her shoe at you."

"She'd have to be paying attention first," Winnie muttered, slowing her step as her mother and Nani marched ahead into the store.

"I bet you she can hear you from back here," Bridget whispered at her side. "She has superpowers."

"Don't I know it," Winnie replied as she entered the store.

Everything in the boutique was new, including the shiny hardwood floors and crystal-clear mirrors, with that fresh, rich smell that only came from new Indian fabrics. All the clothes were packaged in thick plastic, so somehow that scent straight from India was trapped, and released only when the outfit was pulled from the bag.

Winnie looked around at the walls lined with hanging rods filled with covered clothes, and she took a moment to inhale. It was oddly comforting.

"Winnie, come here!" her mother said. She was holding up an electric pink ankle-length skirt while Nani showed off the matching halter top and chuni.

"Oh!" Bridget said. She walked over and ran a hand along the rhinestone-encrusted bodice. "Sparkly."

"It's too pink," Winnie said as she moved closer to them.

"This is the present we wanted to give you," her mother said. "Not this particular outfit, but we know that you have a dance coming up to raise money for your festival. . . ."

"So I am buying you the lengha you'll wear," Nani said as she patted Winnie's cheek.

"Oh," Winnie said. "A lengha? For school?" She'd been hoping to just wear a black dress.

"I think this is perfect for the function," Nani said.

"I don't think that's a good idea."

Winnie's grandmother's and mother's faces grew stony.

"Uh-oh," Bridget said. "I think I see the anklets I want. Off I go!" She slid away to another section of the store.

"Wearing a lengha or a salwar kameez is traditional for Indians attending a function like your dance. What, are you ashamed of your culture?" Nani asked.

"I thought I raised you better than that, Winnie," her mother added.

"And people wonder where I get my drama. Of course

160

I'm not ashamed. Hello, Bollywood movie junkie. But a hot-pink lengha will draw too much attention, and I've been doing enough of that on my own lately."

Winnie's mother sighed. "Beta, that's the *point*. Raj will be there all dressed up."

"That doesn't matter to me."

"Well, it should. What if he tries to make you jealous again and brings Jenny?"

There was no way she'd ever be jealous if Raj took someone else to the dance, and although the idea of looking better than Jenny appealed to her for a hot second, she didn't need to show up her ex and his on-again, off-again girlfriend. "Still, the dance is, like, a few weeks away, and—"

"And you need time in case there are alterations," her mother said. "You know very well alterations can take weeks. Are you really going to say no to me, beta?"

Winnie looked between her mother and her grandmother, who were both staring at her with smiles full of encouragement and excitement. They wanted to do something nice for her. Maybe if she found something plain enough, she wouldn't look too conspicuous. She slowly reached out and touched the lengha.

"If I say yes, I need veto power."

"Done," Nani said. She held the chuni against her chest. "Well? Let's play dress-up."

Winnie smiled. It was no surprise that her love for wardrobe montages came from her family.

After forty-five minutes of trying on clothes that were either too fancy, too colorful, or too gaudy, Winnie pushed the dressing-room curtain aside. She was back in her yoga pants but hadn't put her sneakers on yet.

"Ma, are we almost done? I want to eat at Shalimar's before they close. I could really go for some kebabs right now."

Bridget was nowhere to be found, and Winnie's mother and grandmother weren't even paying attention to her. They were consumed in a conversation with a short, stout woman gripping a worn black leather purse. Dev's mom. The moment of recognition gave Winnie a jolt.

"Hi, Sharda Auntie," Winnie said as she approached the woman.

"Hello, beti, tu kaisi hai?"

"I'm fine, thank you. How are you?"

"Fine, fine, thank you."

"We're getting Winnie an outfit," her mother said. "It's a gift from her nani."

"Oh!" Dev's mother grinned at Winnie. "So nice to have a nani who cares so much, no?"

Winnie nodded. "Yes, absolutely. Ma, I'm sorry to interrupt, but I've tried on everything. I think we should go. . . ."

Winnie's mother made a flicking motion with her fingers. "This girl, nah? So picky. Did you see anything while you were shopping?"

Dev's mother tapped a finger to her lip. "You know, my

friend Jyoti who works here was telling me about the latest parcel from Delhi. Jyoti! Jyoti, come here."

The sales assistant who she called over was painfully thin, with frizzy black hair that was ferociously bound in a thick ponytail. She had a large red bindi pasted to the middle of her forehead. "Can I help you?" she asked in a thick accent.

The women spoke while Winnie forced herself to wait patiently. Jyoti then left to get a few options.

"Ma, where's Bridget?"

"She's upstairs trying on the men's clothes," her mother said. "Something about gender-bending pants. I didn't think they sold those types of pants here."

"I'm going to wait in the fitting room." Winnie slipped behind the curtain and perched on the bench. This night was never going to end unless she did something about it. She reached for her phone and called Dev.

"Hey," Dev said when he picked up the phone. "I'm in the middle of shooting, so you have two minutes before I gotta go."

Winnie heard the sound of people talking in the background, and maybe even bells. "I thought you already finished your movie for the festival," she whispered.

"I'm making some last-minute changes. And why are you whispering?"

"Because I'm in a dressing room, and *your* mother, my mother, my grandmother, and the saleslady are trying to get me to buy an Indian outfit. I don't even *want* to buy an Indian outfit."

"Wait, wait. You're in a fitting room? Naked, possibly? I don't believe you."

She smiled only because she knew that he wasn't there to see it. "Please do something."

"I have no idea why my mother is there, but I can call her if you do one thing for me."

"I'm not taking pictures for you!"

"No, you perv," he said with a laugh. "Go on that date you promised me. On Saturday. We'll go somewhere. Or come to my house and we'll watch movies."

She felt her fingers go numb, and she gripped the phone a little tighter. She didn't want to drop it midswoon. "I thought you'd forgotten."

"I haven't forgotten you in three years, Winnie," he said.

Winnie closed her eyes at the sound of those words and pressed a fist to her beating heart.

"Dev," she said. "This is fast."

"Not for me. I have to go."

"Winnie!" The sound of her name coming from outside the curtain raked on her nerves.

"Dev, call your mom."

"You got it. I'll call . . . as soon as I finish this scene."

"Dev!"

"Just a few minutes," he said, and hung up the phone.

She couldn't decide if she was annoyed or amused by him. She put her phone away. Everything faded out and her eyes locked onto the delicate lengha in Jyoti's arms.

The skirt was bright red with a thick gold border at the bottom. She could already tell that it was so full that if she twirled, the fabric would fan around her. The top was black and belly-baring, with a matching gold border right under the bust line. The sleeves were black and plain. The chuni was a sunset yellow with gold trim. The three different colors shouldn't have worked, but for some reason they melded together perfectly. It was unlike any other combination of color she'd seen in the store.

"This is it," Jyoti said, beaming. "This is perfect for you. With your height and hair, and your curvy midsection, you'll be the most beautiful person at the dance. I'll be right back with some jewelry." She hustled away.

"You like it, beta?"

"I love it. Thanks, Nani. Really. Is it too expensive, though?"

"You let me worry about that. You need to dress like the heroine you were meant to be."

"Here we are," Jyoti said as she presented a felt-lined box filled with different types of jewelry. Dev's mom reached in and pulled out a silver bracelet. The bangle was a thin rope of sterling silver that had two silver balls locking together at the top. A paisley pattern wrapped around the curve of the bracelet, adding a traditional twist to the modern. If Winnie had to wear one bracelet for the rest of her life, the one Dev's mother was holding would be it.

"What a beautiful piece," her grandmother said.

Before Winnie could reply, Bridget called from the staircase. She was wearing a groom's wedding turban, and her arms were full of jewelry boxes. A harried-looking sales associate rushed after her. "Winnie, I found some anklets!"

Thank the gods for best friends, Winnie thought as everyone focused on Bridget.

In the end she got away with just purchasing the lengha and some new jutti flats that matched the outfit's color scheme. Bridget was the one who left with jewelry. On the drive home, no one brought up that amazing bracelet they'd seen. Truthfully, she was grateful they'd all taken the hint that she didn't want to talk about jewelry and prophecies.

But that night, when she was alone in bed, she thought of that perfect silver bracelet again before she drifted off to sleep.

Winnie ran hard and fast through the field, gasping all the way. She felt a weight on her wrist sliding with each step, and she stopped to look down at it.

It was the bracelet. The same one she'd seen in the shop. It fit so perfectly and felt so right. She scanned the horizon and saw the familiar outline of Shah Rukh Khan in the distance. She started running again. Maybe he could tell her what this all meant.

She got closer and closer, heaving with the strength it took to run in the wind. When she was within touching distance, the man turned. Winnie gasped and stumbled. Instead of the face of the Bollywood actor she'd seen so many times before, Dev's face looked back at her.

"Finally," he said, and held out his arms as if waiting for her to run into them.

14

GOLIYON KI RAASLEELA: RAM-LEELA
★★★★★

I'm a purist. Totally not a fan of kissing, intense make-out sessions, or especially *gasp* sex scenes in Bollywood. I think the intensity between the characters is so much better when they have to restrain themselves.

EDIT: I changed my mind.

Winnie pulled the overhead visor down to check her hair and eyeliner for the tenth time. She'd been doing that at every traffic light since she'd left her house twenty minutes ago. She'd just finished patting her loose curls into place when the light changed.

Dev lived in North Brunswick, behind the movie theater that played both American and Indian movies, so she knew how to get to his place easily. She crossed Route 1 and soon reached a small stretch of ranch houses lining a narrow street.

"This is it," she mumbled as she stopped in front of a blue-and-white house. The walkway was lined with flowering bushes, and the door knocker was in the shape of the god Ganesh. The elephant head had a long trunk curved in a U shape.

She grinned and was reaching up to touch the metal detail on the trunk when the door wrenched open. Winnie immediately jumped back, and almost tumbled over the potted plants.

"Hey," Dev said as he leaned against the door in his fitted black shirt. The fabric molded to his chest in a totally-can't-help-but-stare way.

"Hey."

"Come in." He motioned her inside.

"I, uh, brought a couple movie choices for you to pick from." She closed the front door and toed off her shoes, pushing them into the corner with Dev's much larger sneakers. She noticed that a calendar from the Durga Temple in Princeton was tacked to the wall in the foyer. The picture of the goddess Laxmi sitting on a lotus surrounded by a ring of light was framed with sticky notes about dry cleaning and bills.

"Let's take a look," he said, and disappeared through an archway.

"Where are you going?"

"I'm getting drinks."

She followed the sound of his voice and entered a small kitchen painted in sunny yellow.

"Mom isn't here, but she cooked us a feast. Are you hungry? I can heat this food, too."

"Uh, no, not really." They were home alone. So did that mean . . . ? Oh boy. She hadn't shaved her legs above the knee today.

No. No, she wasn't going to go there. If Dev thought he was getting lucky, then he was going to be really, really disappointed.

"Okay," he said, stepping from behind the fridge door. He threw her a bottle of Starbucks mocha iced coffee. She caught it with two hands.

"I could have dropped it!"

"But you didn't."

Winnie rolled her eyes and started shaking the bottle. "I love these things. Thanks."

"I know, and you're welcome."

Before she could ask how he'd known, Dev was picking up a bowl of popcorn, a king-size bag of M&M's, and a bottle of Gatorade, which he tucked under his arm. He rounded the counter and walked down a short hallway.

"The TV room is in the basement." He opened the first door on the right, flicked on the light with his elbow, and jogged down a steep flight of stairs. Winnie followed him much more carefully.

When they got to the bottom, Winnie took in the large beat-up brown couches and spotty beige carpeting. When she turned to the left, she let out a gasp.

She had never seen so much camera equipment in her life. In one tiny section of the basement, Dev had managed to store multiple tripods, camera stands, lenses, cases, headphones, microphones, recorders, and other mechanical devices. A table with three computer screens and multiple towers crowded up against the wall.

"Wow, Dev. That's . . . insane. I may have a lot of movies, but you have a lot of studio equipment." She started walking toward it, but he gripped her arm and gently pulled her back.

"No way. I'm working on my short revision for the festival. You can't touch until I'm done. Come on, give up the movies. Let's see what crap you're going to make me watch today."

"Crap? Excuse me, but I have some of Bollywood's finest work with me. You are going to love this." She pulled a stack of DVDs out of her bag.

"Do you seriously expect me to watch *Hum Aapke Hain Koun*?"

"It's a modern classic," she said.

"No. Next?"

"What? The music is so good. Do you know how many times people have quoted this film? How many weddings reference the dialogue and choreography?"

"Still no. Come on, what other choices do I have?"

"Ugh. Fine." She held up *Kapoor and Sons.* "It's a great movie about family relationships."

"One I've actually seen. My mother makes it a point to watch all the Bollywood movies about cheating dads."

"Oh. Okay, then."

She went through three more movies before getting to

Kabhi Khushi Kabhie Gham. "We are watching this," she said, anticipating his denial. "I don't care what you say—we are going to sit through this entire movie. Why? Because Kajol and Shah Rukh Khan are actors who can teach even the worst critic a thing or two about on-screen chemistry. This movie is beautiful, except for Kareena Kapoor's crying and melodrama scenes. If I have to argue with you through this entire movie, I will."

Dev sighed and held out his hand for the disc.

Winnie gave a victory cheer and plopped down on the couch. She was already reaching for the popcorn when Dev sat next to her after starting the movie.

"Wait, don't do that yet. Here." He opened the bag of M&M's and sprinkled them over the popcorn.

"I was hoping that was what the M&M's were for," Winnie said. "You know, for our first official date, I'd say you hit it out of the park."

"What are you talking about? This is our third date. We went to a carnival, then to a football game, and now we're watching movies. For two movie fans, I'm surprised it took us this long to get here."

Winnie started ticking the dates off on her fingers. "The carnival happened because Henry invited me, and you almost puked on the Ferris wheel—"

"Can we forget about that? Talk about the first-kiss part," he said. "We did that, too."

"The second date was a group thing."

"I gave you my sweatshirt, which you have not given back, by the way."

She had no intention to, either, she thought as she ticked off a third finger. "And we watch movies together on Sundays at the film-club screenings."

"That's when you're not avoiding me," Dev said.

"What? I sat next to you for the last two screenings. And this Sunday, when we're watching the one about escargots, I'll even let you hold my hand. How about that?"

"I still say this is our third date and our first movie date."

Winnie tossed a throw pillow at him. "Semantics."

He caught it deftly and placed it at his side before handing her the popcorn and M&M's. "Let's do this," he said.

She snuggled in to watch the opening scene with Jaya Bachchan playing mom to a growing boy. As the music played, Winnie let the magic take over. The setting, the acting, the dialogue. When a movie was made well, she could feel every emotion that the characters felt, and she was right there with them, hurting, crying, laughing, and yelling. At one point, Dev wrapped an arm around her shoulder and moved in closer.

"I'm glad you're not a talker," Dev said as Shah Rukh Khan's character followed the heroine through a street festival. "I'm not a talker during movies."

"Funny how you have to talk to mention that to me."

He laughed. "You've seen this movie how many times?"

"Doesn't matter. Every time I watch it, I discover—"

"Something new."

"Even when Raj and I were in the good parts of our relationship, he avoided rewatching. I'm glad you get that."

She watched as Dev's eyes narrowed. "Do me a favor and don't compare me to that dipshit, okay?"

He faced the screen, putting distance between them.

"I'm not comparing. I'm just saying that the one person who I thought understood me the most didn't get me at all." She took a deep breath and added, "And the person who I least expected to understand me has been so awesome to me in such a short span of time."

She saw the corner of Dev's mouth curve even as he focused on the movie. Well, that wasn't awkward at all, she thought. Seriously, what was she thinking to say something like that to Dev?

On-screen, Shah Rukh Khan and Kajol's characters were transposed to the beautiful desert in Egypt, where they sang and danced together. When Shah Rukh Khan kissed Kajol's neck, Winnie sighed again. Because she was becoming engrossed in the love story, she was blindsided by the pillow that hit her on the side of the head.

"Hey!"

"I had to make sure you weren't going to start screaming like a fangirl. Are you serious? You're sighing over this stuff? For God's sake, Winnie, they are dancing in *Egypt*. This doesn't happen in real life!"

"Of course it doesn't happen in real life! That's the whole point."

Dev paused the movie. "This I have to hear. If it's not supposed to mimic real life, then what's the point?"

"When you watch a movie like *Star Wars*, is that supposed to mimic our reality?"

"No, that creates a different world, a different reality, but with emotions that audiences in this reality can relate to."

"And that's exactly what these kinds of Bollywood movies do," Winnie said. "They create a separate reality in which singing and dancing become acceptable. And this," she said, waving to the screen, "is the world of Bollywood romance at its finest."

Dev shook his head. "Okay, well, can you please clue me in on your interpretation of the corny song-and-dance routine? Because I'm not exactly seeing what you are."

Winnie rolled her eyes. "It's hard to explain what true romance is like."

Dev laughed so hard he almost rolled off the couch. "You think this dialogue and this singing-and-dancing stuff is true romance?"

"What, you think you can do better than the great Shah Rukh Khan?" She snorted. "I doubt that."

"You know what? Challenge accepted," he said, facing her. He gripped her hands. "I'm excellent at wooing."

"Yeah, okay. This I gotta see."

"Winnie."

"Yes?" She giggled. Dev squeezed her hands in retaliation. "I'm not feeling very wooed, Dev."

"Stop it. Okay." Dev pushed the coffee table away from them with a foot and got down on one knee in front of her. "Winnie, when I first saw you, this giant lens that I've had on my future came into focus. It was like everything was blurry before, and then when you arrived, it was crystal clear."

"Oh. Oh, Dev."

"And I'm not going to lie, it hurt when you left for someone else. But I'm glad you're back and—and, Winnie . . . I don't understand why you love the singing and dancing and Bollywood drama, and I never thought I'd direct choreography, but Winnie Mehta, I would dance for you."

The only sound that Winnie could hear was the pounding of her heart. She wanted to say something, anything. But sometimes words weren't enough. She laid her palms against the cool skin of his cheeks, leaned forward, and touched her lips to his.

Dev's reaction was instantaneous. He pressed against her mouth until she was lying on the couch and he was stretched over her. Then there was his mouth and hers, his chest against hers, and their rushing heartbeats synced.

Holy baby Shah Rukh Khan.

His knee slipped between her legs, and his mouth slanted

against hers. Her thoughts scattered even as she combed her fingers into his hair. She leaned in for another kiss, another touch, to feel him close to her.

Winnie's phone shrilled. She scrambled from under Dev, breathing heavily as she pulled her cell phone out of her bag. The first thought she had was that her mother was calling and that she knew exactly what Winnie was up to.

"Really?" Dev said. "Perfect timing."

The thrill died when Raj's name flashed on the screen, and she groaned. After declining the call, she shoved her phone in her bag, but it started buzzing again.

"Who is it?" Dev asked.

"No one important." She flipped off the sound, but her phone vibrated with a text. She glared at the screen as she read the message.

RAJ: Sorry if you're busy. At the school. Problem with
festival location. They're renovating the theater we always
use.

She hesitated. Raj should be able to deal with it himself. She looked down at Dev, who raised an eyebrow at her. Her phone buzzed a second time.

RAJ: PLEAZZEEE. I NEED YOU. Come down to school.
Committee is here. It's an emergency!!

"What's going on?"

"It's a stupid festival emergency," Winnie said.

Dev groaned. "Seriously? Of course that numbnut would call now. Does he know you're with me?"

"I didn't tell him. It's okay. I'll stay. He can deal on his own."

She patted his leg, and he shifted to give her space. She was about to kiss him again when her phone buzzed for a third time.

"That's it—I'm turning it off."

"Winnie," Dev said. "Listen, if it's an emergency, your mind is going to be on that instead of on me. Why don't we, I don't know, have a rain check or something?"

"But we're only halfway through the movie!"

With a laugh Dev said, "We probably wouldn't watch the rest of it anyway."

Winnie blushed. She should never have checked her phone.

"Dev, I'm sorry."

"Yeah, me too," he said.

Winnie tried to pat her curls into some semblance of order, and then gave up and braided her hair over one shoulder.

"I hope this emergency is worth it," Dev muttered from his position on the couch.

"Me too." Winnie gave him a quick kiss, grabbed her bag, and started up the stairs.

"Hey!" he shouted after her.

"Yeah?"

"You going to the fund-raiser dance with me?"

"I don't know—are you asking?"

"Yeah," he said, sitting up. His smile slipped away. "Are we dating?"

"Keep watching those movies," she said, ignoring his question and the knot in her stomach. "See you in school."

She practically raced out the door and into her car. When she stopped at a red light on Route 1, she pressed her forehead to the steering wheel. No matter how hard she tried to get away from her horoscope, it kept tapping her on the shoulder to remind her that any man other than Raj wasn't for her. The only problem was that she didn't want Raj. She wanted Dev.

On the rest of the ride to the school, she racked her brain for a film comparison that could solve her problem. But she kept drawing a blank, because Dev wasn't part of a Bollywood story to her.

Winnie knew the right thing to do was cut her losses now. Any pain she experienced with Raj would be nothing in comparison to the devastation that she'd experience if Dev broke her heart.

15

HUM DIL DE CHUKE SANAM /
I GAVE MY HEART AWAY, DARLING
★★★★☆

My advice to the heroine in this movie? Sometimes going back to the one you loved in the past is a good thing. And sometimes . . . well, sometimes it's time to move on.

Winnie couldn't help but think about Dev as she walked through the empty school hallways. It had been three weeks since he'd kissed her brainless in his basement, and since then, they'd worked together at the theater, hung out at film-club screenings with Henry and Bridget, and talked about their future. Of course she still had to deal with a gazillion things in her life like school and the festival, but she was happier than she'd been in a long time. She just wished that everyone would believe her. Her grandmother and mother asked questions about Pandit Ohmi's prophecy so much now that Winnie felt like it was the one plot point in her Bollywood movie that didn't have closure.

And of course there was Raj. Winnie hated that he kept

popping up out of nowhere with "emergencies," which is exactly what she told him every time he asked for her help.

Winnie rounded the corner and sighed when she saw him waiting for her in the art studio. Foam boards were propped on easels in a U shape in front of him. The room was empty except for the smell of turpentine and the sound of music playing through the wall-mounted speakers.

"This is the fourth time you've called me over in the last three weeks for some emergency," she said, pushing away from the doorjamb. "First it was a problem with the location, then you couldn't figure out the agenda, and yesterday the website was down. I have no idea why I bother coming."

"Why do you?"

She dropped her backpack on an empty stool and peeled off her jacket. "Maybe it's because I'm hoping in exchange for my time, you'll report Jenny Dickens to the administration for her psycho behavior."

Raj shrugged sheepishly. "She's harmless, but I'm sorry about all the rumors she's spreading. She'll get over it soon, I hope."

"Yeah, because being told that I'm a ho for being with you and with Dev is getting old. She's stalking you, and now she's stalking me and sabotaging. She's like *Swimfan* or an equally atrocious villain."

"What about Shah Rukh Khan in *Fan*?"

Winnie laughed. "Or Kajol in *Gupt*. So far she hasn't gone

psycho like Kajol, but she keeps posting all of these passive-aggressive messages about revenge. That screams *problem* to me."

Raj straightened his sweater vest before tucking his hands in the pockets of his cargo pants. "I'll deal with it, I promise. I feel bad because I wasn't straight with her and didn't tell you how I felt about . . . well, you know."

"I know," Winnie said. She strolled toward the first poster to study it. There was a movie reel with the lead reading the name of the festival. Underneath that, the Princeton University location and the date and time were stamped in gothic lettering. They only had two and a half months to go before the festival.

Raj stepped up behind her and rested his hands on her shoulders. She quickly sidestepped out of his reach.

"Raj . . ."

"Friends can't touch each other?"

"Not if that friend has ulterior motives," she murmured, and moved to the next poster. The background image was of a velvet red curtain. The lettering was simple with glitter edges.

"Let's use this one for the tickets and the posters, while re-branding the website with the same colors and the same artwork scheme. Even though the fund-raiser is next weekend, I think we can get this printed in time for the dance, too."

Raj didn't say anything, and when she faced him, he was smiling.

"What?"

"Nothing. I couldn't pick one, and you decided in seconds."

"Well, it's probably because I spent most of the summer thinking about this in my spare time. Okay, you got this from here. See you later."

Before she could leave, Mr. Reece appeared in the doorway. "Winnie. Raj."

"Mr. Reece," Winnie said. "It's been a while since you've come to one of our events. I was going to send you a meme of the *Millennium Falcon* just so you'd remember my name."

"I don't understand why it's so hard for you to learn the difference between *Star Wars* and *Star Trek*. You picked up physics easily enough. Anyway, Ms. Sealy said that you two were taking up her spare art room for the festival, so I came down to check in. Are we still on track?"

"Winnie has actually covered for me on a lot of the details," Raj said.

"Raj, we talked about this."

"I know," he said with a shrug. "But I have a lot going on. I told you it was too much work for one of us to handle, even with the committees taking care of the venue decorating, the movie submissions, and the judging."

"I offered to lend a hand so I can show leadership initiative," Winnie said with a smile. She was grateful that Raj was helping her, but when Mr. Reece arched an eyebrow, she wondered if their joint efforts were working. "I'm handling it, Mr. Reece," she continued. "We have some time until the festival, and the fund-raiser is booked in the school ballroom for next weekend. The film-club funds are being used for the food, and we have an alumnus playing DJ, so we're saving money there. I'm operating completely within the rules of how a club should work."

Mr. Reece smiled, the first genuine smile she'd seen from him since he became the film-club faculty advisor. "And the master-class status?"

Since Mr. Reece was looking at her and not Raj, Winnie answered. "I've coordinated with the Princeton film club. As long as Gurinder Chadha shows up, we'll be good to go."

He headed for the door. "Good job, Ms. Mehta. Maybe you deserve a co-chair position after all," he said over his shoulder.

When Winnie couldn't hear his footsteps anymore, she gave in to the temptation to squeal and started jumping up and down.

"See? I knew you could do it," Raj said. "Sorry I haven't been as helpful."

She shook her head. "You've done a lot, and I get why you can't push Reece too hard. You have to get into your Boston school and need the film festival on your application. You technically don't have to help your ex, so I appreciate it."

"Appreciate it enough to come with me for a quick side trip to the auditorium?" he said.

"What for?"

"Come and see."

"I have plans tonight," she said to Raj. "It has to be quick."

He grinned. "As quick or as long as you want."

"Fine," she said with a sigh. "Why not? For old times' sake."

She noticed the flash of sadness in his eyes, but didn't comment as he led her to the auditorium. When he opened the double doors, Winnie saw the huge white screen that spanned the stage.

Raj stepped aside and motioned toward it with a bow. "After you."

"What are you up to?" she asked as she headed down the aisle.

"I arranged it before you met me in the art room. I was hoping you could watch something with me before you left."

A small projector was placed in front of the stage, pointing at the screen. Next to it was Raj's laptop. She moved to sit in the front row, but he stopped her.

"The world may sit in the front row—"

"But Indians sit in the back," she said with a laugh. "Or people who know that's how you get the whole picture." She grabbed the center seat in the center row. Raj set something up on his laptop, and when a movie started playing, Winnie's palms grew damp. This felt . . . wrong.

Raj sat next to her as the opening scene started rolling.

"*Dil To Pagal Hai*?" she said as her uneasiness grew.

"Yeah. It's been a while since we've seen this."

"For good reason. I'm sorry—I can't stay, Raj. I have to go."

"Why?" he asked, standing when she did.

"Because you're doing this to remind me of my destiny, and I don't like it. I don't know how many times I have to tell you that the prophecy is mine to believe in. I get to decide if I want to be with someone who fits Pandit Ohmi's prediction."

"Winnie," he said with a laugh. "It's just a movie. Our favorite movie, in fact. And maybe it was because it reminded you so much about the prophecy, but we still had fun watching it over the years. It's the only exception to my rule about never rewatching a movie if I don't have to."

"But that's in the past," she said. "I know you've been calling me so we can spend more time together, but this is too much."

Raj ran his hands through his hair and frowned. "I'm trying here, Winnie. I haven't even mentioned that I think you should still come to Boston with me instead of New York—"

"Yeah, well, you just did. I can't believe you and I dated for all these years and you never thought I'd make it as a film critic." She could feel herself getting worked up, and her anger mixed with hurt.

"Having a blog doesn't make you a film critic," he snapped.

"That's it. I'm done." She grabbed her bag and headed for the door.

Raj called out after her. "Wait. I'm sorry. Winnie, I'm

sorry. I'm frustrated that you're dragging your heels, that's all. I'll make it up to you. Next weekend when we go to the fund-raiser dance—"

She stopped and turned on her heel in the aisle. "'We'? What do you mean by 'we'?"

"Well, I figured I'd pick you up, we'd go to the dance early to make sure everything is set up, and then we could eat and drink for the rest of the night. That's how we always planned it."

"But we're not *together*."

"I know, but we're going to the dance as friends, right? We've gone to every school dance together. The fund-raiser shouldn't be an exception."

"Raj. I'm going with Dev."

"Come on. You can't be serious. We have *three years* together. What do you even see in Dev? He's such a smug prick, thinking he's better than everyone."

"Hey!" Winnie yelled. "Don't talk about him like that. You don't know him. You're the one who saw he liked me freshman year and went behind your friend's back to date me. If I'd known . . ."

Holy baby Shah Rukh Khan. She hadn't meant to say that.

Raj stood, stone-faced. When he didn't deny the claim, she knew more than ever that nothing was going to be the same.

"How could you?" she whispered.

"He wasn't for you," Raj said calmly. "We were meant to

be, Winnie. Bracelet, name, everything. And we still are. It's your prophecy, but I'm part of it."

"You only gave me that bracelet because you thought that's what was expected of you, Raj. What does that say about you and me? And it was really easy for you to go to Jenny when I wasn't around during the summer. The minute we met again at the first film-club meeting—no, when you heard Dev comment on how I looked at that meeting—all of a sudden you were interested again."

"That's not true."

Winnie walked to him, stood on her tiptoes, and kissed his smooth cheek. "If I don't see you in the halls, I'll meet up with you next week before the fund-raiser to help the committee set up."

She walked away, ignoring his protests, his apologies, everything. Raj was behind her now, and she needed to start acting like she believed it.

Winnie wore a white tunic top, a white chuni, and white balloon pants. Her frizzy hair fell in waves past her shoulders. She stood in the middle of a mustard field, a farmhouse in the distance. The sound of a cowbell and familiar chords playing on a mandolin rang over the wide spaces. There was nothing but blue skies, the smell of fresh, clean air, and music.

"Shah Rukh Khan, if you think I wouldn't recognize one of your most famous scenes from Dilwale Dulhania Le Jayenge, then you're crazy!"

She started running toward the sound, hoping that she could find him, find the one person who might be able to provide her with some insight into her life. She stopped when the field cleared and she saw the actor wearing a leather jacket and carrying a polished mandolin.

"Why, hello there, señorita," he said with a bow.

Winnie ran just as gracelessly as Kajol had, and dove straight into his arms.

"You have no idea how happy I am to see you," she said.

"I came to tell you two things," he said, stepping back.

"Okay, hit me."

"If you walk on the wrong path, then maybe in the beginning you'll achieve a lot of happiness and success, but in the end you'll lose. If you walk on the right path, then maybe at the start you'll get rejections at every step, but in the end you'll always win."

Winnie threw her hands up and got caught in her chuni. She pulled the shawl off her face and crossed her arms over her chest. "Seriously? The only advice you're giving me is a movie quote? I thought we were past that."

"Think about it," he said with his signature shaky laugh.

"If I travel the wrong path, then I'll lose, but if I travel the right path, there will be pitfalls but eventually I'll win.

Okay, so even though Dev isn't part of my prophecy, things are going to suck for a bit, but in the end I'm making the right decision?"

Shah Rukh Khan backed up even farther, arms spread wide. "I don't know, señorita. You tell me. It's your life, your destiny. After all, I know how much izzat means to a woman."

Respect. Her mother and father had spoken about izzat when they'd told her to pay back Raj. That was another line from the movie.

"Wait, so even if I don't love Raj, I should still respect that he could be my hero?"

Shah Rukh Khan didn't say anything else. He pulled the strap of his mandolin over his shoulder, resumed playing the tune from the movie, and faded into the distance, leaving Winnie alone again.

Winnie woke up slowly, letting out a shuddering breath. "This sucks," she said in the dark. She'd been asleep for only a short period of time before the dream interrupted her rest.

After ten minutes of tossing and turning, she was still wide awake. With a groan, she got up and pulled her copy of *Dilwale Dulhania Le Jayenge* off the shelf. It took only another moment of debating before she opened her bedroom door and went downstairs, where the sounds of conversation mixed with Indian soap operas.

"Winnie? I thought you went to sleep," her mother said.

"I did, but I had a weird dream again."

"I hope it involved an eligible bachelor," Nani said.

"Not unless you consider Shah Rukh Khan to be the bachelor." She held up her copy of the movie she'd dreamed about. "I was going to watch this alone. It's long, but anyone interested?"

Winnie's father raised his hand like a student. "Yash Raj Films at its finest."

"This calls for more . . . ah, lassi," Nani said, holding up her steel tumbler.

"You both are going to be tired for work and school tomorrow," Winnie's mother said. "It's already eleven."

"So?" they replied.

"Okay, then. Just this once and only because I haven't seen it in a long time, either."

Winnie grinned and went over to the TV to put in the movie. If she was going to have another sleepless night, she couldn't think of a better way to stay awake than to watch movies with her family.

16

KUCH KUCH HOTA HAI /
SOMETHING HAPPENS
★★★★☆

I would like for Bollywood movies to address the true awkwardness that happens right before the party. Realistically, the heroine probably stabs herself in the eye with her mascara wand and her parents make her take a thousand selfies to post in the "India Family" WhatsApp group. The struggle is real, guys.

DEV: Time for another date.

WINNIE: I'm not losing count of our dates here. Don't be late. <3

"You're not thinking about *him,* are you?" Bridget asked from the v-chat screen on her dresser. They weren't getting ready together because Henry was going to pick up Bridget from her place and Dev was driving Winnie.

"I'm not thinking about who?" Winnie asked as she smoothed a hand over her curls.

"Raj," Bridget said. "You're not thinking about him, right? Because you got really quiet really fast when I asked if your parents are finally okay with you and Dev. Now you look annoyed. Looking annoyed will crease your makeup. You hardly ever wear any, so you need to keep that flawless look."

Winnie chose to ignore the makeup comment. "No, I'm not thinking about Raj. Well, sort of. Today when I saw him while we were setting up the ballroom, he looked so sad. I don't know why."

"Maybe it's because he's all about getting his way. He wants the girl, the school, the future. I heard a couple days ago that he's going to the dance with Jenny Dickens even though she was being all crazy and spreading rumors about you guys. I bet you it's because he's trying to save face because no one else wants to go out with him now."

Bridget disappeared offscreen, and Winnie heard rustles of fabric. When she returned to her spot in front of the camera, Winnie gasped at the vision she made. The stunning shimmer of the gown wasn't nearly as bright as the sparkle in Bridget's eyes.

"Oh my God, you look so beautiful! I think you look even more stunning now that you're with Henry. You know, I'm going to keep reminding you that I'm the reason you and Henry are together." She patted her shoulder. "Good job, self."

Bridget rested her hands on her hips and leaned in closer to the computer screen. She said in her best British accent, "'Oh! Lizzy, why am I thus singled from my family, and blessed above them all! If I could but see you as happy!'"

"Okay, Jane, no *Pride and Prejudice* quotes allowed

tonight. I don't have a lot of brain space to spare for a witty retort."

"It's better than a *Say Anything* quote."

"We really need to get you to watch more eighties movies. That's not even the best one."

"I'm going to pretend you didn't say that."

"Yeah, yeah."

Winnie walked over to her bed and looked down at the lengha that her grandmother had purchased for her. She had been doing stomach crunches for weeks to prepare for the belly-baring top. Hopefully it would look as good, if not better, when she slipped it on.

"By the way, Henry texted and said that the ballroom looks awesome. I'm assuming that's because you were hovering this morning."

"Did you really expect me to let the decorating committee do their own thing?" she asked as she slipped into the skirt.

"Are you going to make a lot of money for the festival, or is this all for nothing?"

Winnie put on her top, and then twisted and struggled to pin the chuni to her shoulder as the final part of her outfit. "With ticket sales? We got this in the bag. We have more than enough."

"That's so awesome—Whoa. Winnie."

Winnie had stepped in front of the camera again. "What?

Do I look bad? If it sucks, I'll wear something else. I've got a backup."

Bridget shook her head, eyeing her up and down. "You look . . . like a Bollywood diva."

"I what?"

Bridget nodded. "Check yourself out!"

Winnie walked over to the mirror hanging over her closet door. Her reflection was like a jolt to her system. The lengha was made for her body. Her cheeks warmed, and she couldn't help but smile at the almost surreal image of herself staring back from the mirror. Thankfully it was the exact reaction she'd been hoping for. With her feet sparkling in jeweled juttis, the lengha made her appear more . . . feminine.

She flipped her hair over one shoulder. "I do look good. Okay, I have the jewelry, the shoes, the hair, and the outfit. What do you think about adding a final touch? Bindi or no bindi?"

"Definitely bindi," Bridget said.

Winnie walked over to the drawer that held her jewelry and bindis. When she opened it, she saw the twisted silver bracelet sitting on top. She reached in and ran a finger over the ornate design. She'd worn that bracelet everywhere for almost a year. It wasn't nearly as perfect as the bracelet she'd seen in the Indian shop, but it had meant something. She kept forgetting to take it to school so she could give it to Raj. She couldn't make excuses any longer. Right after the fund-raiser dance, she'd hand it off with a check for what she owed him and they'd be square.

"Yo! What are you doing?"

"Oh, I'm finding a bindi," she said, pushing the bracelet aside and out of her mind. She took a small white square envelope from her dresser drawer. Lifting the envelope flap, she exposed five artfully displayed bindis stuck with a simple adhesive to a thin sheet of plastic. Winnie peeled off a deep red bindi in a paisley design with a jewel in the center. She stood in front of the mirror and, holding her breath, stuck it on what she hoped was the center of her forehead. After a second she let go. The little sticker managed to pull her entire outfit together.

"What do you think?" she asked, returning to Bridget.

"I think you're going to make everyone look horrible compared to your fabulousness."

"Thanks, bestie," she said with a grin. She waved at the computer. "See you in a bit?"

Bridget nodded. "Sooner than you think. Have fun with Dev!"

After taking one more look at herself in the full-length mirror, Winnie grabbed her clutch and headed downstairs. Dev was supposed to be there in half an hour, but first she had to endure the endless pictures her parents would take of her.

"Mom, Dad, I'm ready," Winnie called out as she held up her lengha and carefully walked downstairs.

Her mother and grandmother entered from the kitchen together.

"Come, let me see," her mother said.

Winnie stopped and posed on the last step. "Well?" she said. "How do I look?"

She didn't have to ask, because she saw her mother's and grandmother's smiles spread, creasing the happy lines in their cheeks.

"Kitni soni lagti hai," Nani said.

"Of course she looks beautiful," her mother replied. "She's my beti, no? Come. Let's take some pictures. Let me get your father. The man can't leave his newspaper for two minutes."

"I'm here," he said, walking into the foyer. "I heard you cursing me rooms away."

He stopped when he saw Winnie standing at the bottom of the stairs. "You remind me of how your mother looked on our wedding day."

"Aw, thanks, Daddy."

"One word of advice. Make sure the same thing doesn't happen to you that happened to your mother."

"What was that?"

"After she looked so angelic at our wedding, she morphed into a shrew."

Nani roared in laughter and almost dropped her drink, while Winnie's mother glared at both her mother and her husband.

"Muma, he's talking about your daughter!"

"I know," Nani said, laughing. "That is why I think it is so funny. It is so true!"

She held out her hand and Winnie's father slapped it. The whole scene was so absurd that Winnie couldn't help but grin.

"Let us take our pictures and let the girl have fun," Winnie's father said.

They stood in front of the staircase like they did for every important family picture, and waited while Nani adjusted her glasses and set up her iPhone. Mom took a little bit longer to prep since she usually wanted to share pictures on Facebook, on Instagram, and with the family chat groups.

"I'm proud of you, beta," her father said after the first picture. "You've set yourself a goal and tried to pursue it with honesty. No matter what happens, remember if you've done everything right, then you'll get what you deserve in the end."

"Thanks, Daddy. That means a lot."

By the time they were done with at least three sets of pictures of everyone, the doorbell rang.

"It's Dev. Go away," she said, waving at her parents and grandmother. No one budged from their spot. With a sigh, she walked to the front door, rubbing her damp palms together. She was going to her film club's fund-raiser dance with a guy she was crazy about. This was not a BFD . . . right?

She opened the door on the second ring. Dev stood on the stoop, bathed in the yellow glow of the outdoor lights.

He wore black dress pants, dress shoes, and a long kurta sewn in black with gold threadwork at the throat and wrists.

"Hey," he said as his eyes bulged. "You look . . . wow. Seriously. Wow."

Winnie crossed an arm over her stomach and gripped her elbow. "Um, thanks. You look great, too. I really didn't think you'd wear the Indian clothes."

"Well, my mom saw your lengha thing and suggested that I wear this. I have to admit, I'm really happy she was there with you that day. Now everyone will know you're with me."

"And everyone will know you're with me. Let me grab my bag." She turned and almost ran into her parents. Her grandmother stood behind them.

"Winnie? Aren't you going to let Dev in the house?" her mother said. "We need a picture of the two of you together."

"No."

"Vaneeta," she said, her eyes narrowed. "Move."

She opened the door a bit wider. "Fine. Dev, my parents and grandmother want to say something embarrassing."

She heard him cough, but thankfully he stepped into the foyer without protest. "Hi, Aunties, Uncle. How are you?"

They nodded and said hello. Dev shook hands with Winnie's father.

"How is your mother, beta?"

"Fine," Dev replied. "Thanks for asking, Auntie. She had fun at your pooja and when you shopped together."

Winnie's mom clasped her hands together with a laugh.

"It was fun, no? I'm so glad we ran into her. You must bring her for dinner sometime."

The conversation continued as Winnie and Dev were smoothly ushered into position in front of the staircase for another round of pictures. After two sets, Winnie had had enough.

"Okay, this chitchat is great, but we have to go. Bye."

Before Winnie could follow Dev, her grandmother tugged her arm.

"Winnie," she said softly. "I know that you are struggling with your prophecy—"

"Oh, Nani, please, not tonight. I just want to have a good time."

"Hush. I know you don't understand your prophecy, but I want you to know that I think with Dev, it'll come true in the end. I see it now." She patted Winnie on the shoulder and motioned her through the door.

Winnie wasn't sure how to process Nani's comment, so she nodded and followed Dev outside.

When the door closed behind them, Winnie said, "Dear gods, what happened to Indian humility and not meeting a boyfriend until it's like marriage or whatever? My parents are weird. Sorry."

"Don't worry about it. Ready to go?" Dev said. He motioned to the end of the driveway, and for the first time, Winnie noticed the limo. The massive white stretch took up nearly the entire length of the front of her house.

She almost fell out of her juttis. "What the . . . ?"

Dev pressed a hand against the strip of exposed skin at her back. "That, Vaneeta Mehta, is your chariot."

Winnie looked up at him and then at the limo. "Dev. I— I don't know what to say."

He led her down the front steps and to the end of the driveway. When they got to the back door, Dev stepped in front of it and slipped his hands around her waist. "Tonight's important for all of us in film club, but especially for you. So I wanted every part of tonight to be important. There is one thing you should know, though."

"Oh?"

"We won't be alone."

She heard a sound come from the limo and tried to peer around him to see what was inside.

"Dev?"

He held her hands in his and brought her knuckles to his lips. "You really do look amazing tonight, Vaneeta Mehta. But I don't think I can handle acting out your fairy-tale romance all night, which is why I brought reinforcements."

He reached behind him and pulled on the door handle. She heard screaming from inside the car and saw two familiar faces.

"Surprise!" Bridget and Henry yelled.

"You guys!" she said, laughing. She looked up at Dev. "I don't care what you say—you've got this Bollywood romance thing down."

He leaned down for a quick kiss. "You deserve it."

She slipped inside the vehicle with Dev right behind her. This was what she'd hoped her senior year would be like, she thought. Spending Saturday nights with friends and with a guy she chose for herself. Destiny couldn't stop her tonight no matter what was written in the stars.

17

MAIN HOON NA / I'M HERE FOR YOU
★★★★☆

I admit it. I automatically give extra points to a Bollywood movie that has
at least one phenomenal group dance number. Item songs featuring a
scantily clad woman dancing in front of leering men do not count.

Winnie thought the decorating committee should get jobs on
a Sanjay Leela Bhansali film, because they were that good.
Although she'd helped throughout the process, watching
their vision come to life was amazing. A red carpet connected
one end of the foyer to the ballroom. A large backdrop with
the festival logo was set up in one corner, and she could hear
the DJ spinning remixes through the open double doors.

"Hey, you," Laura said from the front table. "You look
awesome!"

"Thanks! You too. How are we doing on money?"

Laura tilted her head toward the tin box, which held a wad
of cash. "The presales were great, but the sales at the door
are incredible! You did such a terrific job with this. Everyone
knows it was you. Really. Congratulations."

Winnie leaned down and gave her a hug. "Thanks. Do you have someone to switch off with you so you can dance, too?"

She nodded. "Jenny Dickens is supposed to take over."

Winnie plastered a wide smile on her face. How Jenny had managed to take on a volunteer position for the festival was beyond her. Raj must have approved it without Winnie knowing. "Perfect! Have fun, okay?"

Laura nodded and started collecting tickets from the next person in line. "Most def. Oh! Mr. Reece was looking for you. He's inside. See you later!"

Dev grabbed her hand and tugged her in through the open double doors. "Come on, let's check out the food."

"The food is *fantastic*. I picked the caterers myself. But did you hear Laura? Reece is looking for me. What do you think he wants to talk about?"

"There is only one way to find out." He looked up at the dangling stars and streamers from the ceiling. "This is like a perfect set for a Bollywood dance number . . . or a Woody Allen movie."

She tugged his hand. "Wait, I think I'm hearing things. Did Dev Khanna suggest a Bollywood dance number, or was that my imagination?"

He grinned down at her. In the dim light of the ballroom and over the blaring music from the DJ, she could hear him clearly. "Don't you wish someone would start dancing right now?"

She laughed and shoved him in the arm. "Depends on

the dancer. I feel bad for the normal crowd here, though. The South Asian, African, jazz, ballet, contemporary, and hip-hop teams from school all bought tickets. Anyway, where did Bridget and Henry go? Didn't they say they were grabbing seats?"

Before the words left her mouth, Winnie spotted Bridget waving from a table at the side of the room. Winnie linked fingers with Dev and pulled him along to join their friends.

"I've been to every fund-raiser event for film club, and this has to be the best one yet," Bridget said.

"Thanks, Bridge."

Henry lifted a chicken wing and waved it at her. "Get some food," he said. "This stuff is awesome." His suit coat was already off and draped over his chair, and the white sleeves of his button-down shirt were rolled up to his elbows. A green T-shirt peeked out at the nape of his neck.

"The Hulk?" Winnie asked.

"Green Lantern," he replied.

"I think I know who that is."

"We can discuss his choice of superhero T-shirts when we get back," Dev said. "Shall we?"

"We shall," Winnie replied as he led her to the buffet table.

Over the course of half an hour, she ate and laughed with her friends. She waved to other people she went to school with and shook the hands of teachers who were told by other members of the film club that she'd been responsible for putting the fund-raiser dance together. The music got louder and the room darker with more people moving to the center of the room.

Just as she finished her second soda and Dev finished the last bit of pasta on her plate, she felt a tap on her shoulder. She looked up at a smiling Mr. Reece.

"Ms. Mehta, you look dashing this evening."

She stood up and eyed Mr. Reece's tailcoat and bow tie. He couldn't have looked more movie-star double than he did at that moment. "Mr. Reece, Laura mentioned you were looking for me. Sorry, I got caught up. Love the bow tie."

He preened. "Thank you. May I speak with you for a second?"

She nodded and moved with him to a corner of the room.

"Congratulations," he said once they could hear each other. "With your work on the master class and the fund-raiser, you've definitely shown that you're a capable leader who goes above and beyond when necessary."

"Mr. Reece?"

"I know you weren't happy when I enforced the school rules, but that's my job as an educator. It was also a way to push you to be the leader I knew you could be. Yesterday I spoke with the dean and asked him for an exception. You've earned the role as festival chair and film-club president. Congratulations. You can have your title, and I'd be happy to write you a letter of recommendation for NYU."

"For real?" she said, her pulse racing. "This isn't a joke to get back at me for all the *Star Wars* pranks, is it?"

"It's real, but I'd appreciate it if you wouldn't do that anymore."

Winnie squealed and launched herself at Mr. Reece, giving him a bone-crushing hug. "Thank you, Mr. Reece! I promise I'll make you proud."

He managed to detangle from her and said, "Raj and I agree. You deserve the honor to speak on behalf of the film club *and* the festival tonight. I'll introduce you and thank the teachers for being here tonight; then you can take it away."

"Of course. I'm ready. I mean, I can do this. Sure thing."

"Okay, meet me on the left side of the stage in five minutes."

Winnie hadn't prepared a speech, but she nodded, and after sweating it out with Dev, Bridget, and Henry, she approached the stage, where Mr. Reece was already waiting for her. The DJ saw them and started to fade the music.

Mr. Reece jogged up the side steps and waited for Winnie to join him. When they stood side by side, he reached for the microphone and called for everyone's attention. He had to repeat himself twice before the room quieted.

"Thank you all for coming. For those who don't know me, I'm Mr. Reece, the faculty advisor for the film club this year. On behalf of the entire film club, we want to extend our appreciation to you for purchasing fund-raiser tickets." After he acknowledged faculty, he turned to Winnie. "Now I want to introduce you to one of your classmates, who is responsible for coordinating this entire event—Ms. Winnie Mehta!"

The clapping sounded like a thunderous roar. Winnie heard music in her head as she took the microphone from Mr. Reece. It was heavier than she expected. She looked at her friends, the teachers, and the other students. In the middle of the smiling faces, she spotted Raj standing toward the rear of the room, his hands shoved in his pockets. She faltered for a bit, switching the microphone from one sweaty hand to another. When his gaze clashed with hers, he crossed his arms and looked away.

She shook her head as she tried to piece together the words she wanted to say. When she heard Mr. Reece clear his throat next to her, she started.

"Thanks, everyone. The film festival is going to be a success, so I really hope you come out again to see movies made by students here and across the country. The club couldn't have thrown such a party without the help of some amazing people. The decorating committee set up this gorgeous ballroom." She briefly went through the names of each committee and waited while everyone cheered and clapped.

Winnie waved a hand toward the DJ. "And before I get off this stage and let you enjoy the rest of your night, I want to thank our alumnus DJ Ricky Jackson for spinning for us all night!" This time the cheers accompanied music. She faced the audience, expecting the music to stop so she could end her mini speech. Instead the music grew louder and mixed with something that sounded strangely familiar. She looked over at the DJ box and goggled when she saw Henry behind the turntables instead.

"Wha—"

He tilted his head at Winnie and cranked up the volume. The room dimmed, and Winnie turned toward Mr. Reece to ask him if he knew what was going on, but her faculty advisor had abandoned her.

The beat morphed into an Indian song so familiar that the microphone slipped from her hands and landed with a sharp crack on the stage floor.

Her mouth fell open as a spotlight illuminated a figure in the middle of the dance floor.

Dev.

He was wearing a fedora. Indian guys only wore fedoras when they were about to bust out some really cheesy Michael Jackson moves.

Dev did a pelvic thrust and a mini moonwalk to a drumbeat right before the chorus started. Classic Michael.

He transitioned into an arm wave before popping, locking, and pointing at her with a wink.

The crowd was cheering, fists pumping with the music, even though only a handful of people in the ballroom understood the lyrics. Dev had an innate rhythm that Winnie had never expected. A lot of Indian guys danced, but this was Dev! The same Dev who mocked her love for Bollywood dance numbers. Yet there he was, in the middle of the floor, killing it.

He ran forward, fell to his knees, and skidded to a halt in front of her with outstretched arms. She knew the song and the dance that accompanied it better than anyone. This was the part where the girl jumped in and started dancing, too. She leaned down and whispered, "What do you think you're doing?"

He stood and grabbed her hand, tugging her off the stage. She fell into his arms, and before she could regain her equilibrium, Dev was spinning her close.

"How's this for Bollywood hero?" he said.

She watched the crowd twirl around her as she moved. Dev let go of her hand, and she managed to stop before crashing into a nearby table. When she looked toward Dev again, she was smacked in the face with another surprise.

He had backup dancers. She saw Jai and the South Asian dance team move in synchronized movements around them. She rubbed her eyes to make sure she wasn't imagining things, but there they were. Dev and the team followed the same choreography as in the movie.

Bridget appeared at her side and gave her arm a push. "Dev wanted to do this for you. This is your song, girl! He's telling you that he's more important than some stupid prophecy ever could be. Are you really going to stand here, gaping and shocked, while the one guy who actually cares more than

Raj ever could, more than any guy ever has, dances to get your attention?"

Winnie looked over at Dev, whose smile was wavering. He was dancing for her, probably feeling even more embarrassed than she did. She had to give him points for being unique. Winnie reached for Dev, and he was right there waiting for her.

She moved with him to the music, and the sound of screams and cheers was so loud that she almost couldn't hear herself think. Dev grinned at her, and in the final chorus, others joined the dance floor, until there were bodies everywhere, bumping together, jumping and moving to the sound of her favorite song.

Winnie gripped Dev's shoulders, and he came to a stop, took off his fedora, and dropped it on her head. He leaned in close, pressed his cheek to hers, and wrapped his arms around her waist.

"I think I understand why Bollywood movies have songs," he said. "They understand that sometimes people feel so much they have to sing and dance about it. Winnie, no one else makes me want to sing and dance like you do. No one else *could* get me to sing and dance. It's taken three and a half years for me to get your attention, but now that you're looking at me, I want you to know that I'll make sure every day we have together is just as filmi as the next."

He framed her face in his hands. The lights pulsed and

the music thrummed around them as Winnie watched Dev's mouth and listened to his muffled words. They poured through her heart and brightened every part of her.

She gripped his wrists. "I have to tell you something."

Dev leaned his forehead against hers. The fedora tilted up under his sweet gesture. "What?"

"Screw filmi. The real thing with you is so much better." Winnie reached up and kissed him. He opened his mouth, and they melted closer together. Despite the number of people who jostled them, they stayed connected, with the music, with their feelings, and with each other. For the first time in so long, Winnie truly felt whole again, when she hadn't even known that a part of her had been missing.

The crowd parted behind Dev, and she saw in the distance Raj watching her, near the door of the ballroom. Their eyes met again, and Winnie's heart thudded in her chest. He looked brokenhearted, but Winnie couldn't go to him. Not anymore.

Before she turned away, Jenny Dickens, in a black sheath dress, stepped up behind Raj and curled a hand over his shoulder. She smirked and led Raj out the ballroom doors.

"What is it?" Dev said, looking over his shoulder, but Raj and Jenny had already left.

"Nothing," she said. "No one. What are we going to do now?"

Dev leaned forward and kissed the tip of her nose. "Dance?"

"Yes," she said with a laugh. "Let's dance!" She spotted

Bridget and Henry dancing with a few others at the edge of the floor. When Winnie waved, they burst through the crowd and surrounded them. Henry pounded Dev on the back, and Bridget hugged Winnie. The music changed, and this time the DJ played the Bollywood "Breakup Song." Laughing, Winnie and Dev changed up their crazy dance moves.

Dev was with her every step of the night, as Winnie moshed, bhangra-ed, and joined the conga line. When some of the students cleared off tables, Winnie found herself hoisted on top of one and pushed toward the center of the dance floor.

She heard people chanting her name over the pounding music and she scanned the crowd, illuminated in brief bursts of light. The only face she was able to see clearly was Dev's. He grinned up at her.

As every cell of her body danced in sync, she felt her heart pounding in her chest, and without regret, she gave it to Dev. She closed her eyes and fell into his waiting arms. Her life couldn't be any more perfect than this.

18

KHAMOSHI / SILENCED
★★★☆☆

No matter how many movies I watch, I always forget that things have to get a LOT worse before they can get better.

Winnie collapsed at a lunch table on Monday morning and dropped her brown paper bag in front of her. She was exhausted, both from responding to the messages everyone was sending and from the cleanup after the fund-raiser, which had taken all of Sunday.

She folded her arms on the table and rested her head against them with a groan. She'd forgotten that she had to work tonight, too. When the film festival ended, she'd have a lot more time to focus on things like homework, work, movie reviews, and the new guy in her life. Right now she just had to get through the next seven weeks.

"Hey, superstar," Bridget said from next to her. Winnie felt the bench shift and the brush of her best friend's hand against her shoulder.

"I'm not a superstar," she said into the crook of her elbow. "Don't jinx it. I'm happy. A little stressed, but that's it."

"Dev's giving you a workout, huh?"

Winnie's head shot up, and she glared at Bridget, who wiggled her eyebrows. "I could say the same thing about Henry. You guys disappeared early from the dance. We didn't get your text messages until Dev and I took the limo home by ourselves."

Bridget's cheeks reddened. "I don't make out in the back-seat of a car for two hours and tell. My AV nerd has some moves."

Winnie laughed and hugged her friend. "I'm happy you're happy."

"I'm happy *you're* happy," Bridget replied. "This is the first time you've really let loose since Raj and you started going south."

"And the funny thing is, I feel better than I did before we broke up. Like even the good times with him, as distant a memory as they may be, don't compare to how . . . I don't know, grounded I am right now."

"Well, there are probably other reasons for that."

They were still laughing when Jessica came up to the table. Her face was white as a sheet, and instead of the happy glow she'd had when she attended the dance over the weekend, her lips were drawn, and her eyes were bloodshot.

"Hey," Winnie said. "What's up?"

"Winnie, Mr. Reece needs to see you in his office right now." She handed her a pass.

Winnie looked down at the pass and then back at Jessica. Reece only gave passes if the matter was a big deal and if it might make her miss her next class.

"Girl, what happened?" Bridget said, waving to the seat across from her. "You look like you were forced to watch the Disney Channel for fifteen hours in a row."

Jessica looked left and right before she sat down. "The fund-raiser money from yesterday is missing, and Jenny Dickens is telling everyone Dev took it."

"*What?*" Bridget and Winnie said in unison.

"What do you mean it's missing?" Winnie asked.

Jessica tilted her head toward the other side of the room and cupped a hand over her mouth. "You know how Laura was in charge of ticket sales at the door, right? Well, Jenny took over for the rest of the night, and she was supposed to give the money to Mr. Reece. Except she told Mr. Reece after the dance that she gave it to Dev because he said he was in charge of the money."

"That's impossible! Dev was with me," Winnie said. "We went home after the last song, and came back to school the next morning to clean up."

"You guys shouldn't have allowed Jenny anywhere near the fund-raiser," Bridget said.

"It wasn't me."

"I know you guys didn't do it," Jessica said. "I saw both of you. But Jenny is saying that Dev took the money and promised to give it to Mr. Reece. Dev is denying it, obviously."

"This is such bullshit," Winnie said, crumpling the pass in her fist.

Jessica shrugged. "I know. It's her word against Dev's."

Winnie reached down for her backpack and, after a few tries, managed to unzip the front pocket. When she checked her phone, she saw three texts from Dev, and her stomach twisted with fresh nausea.

"I've gotta go," she said, and grabbed her things before bolting.

She ran down the halls and tried to think what Raj and Jenny had done with the money and the proof they'd shown to Reece to make him believe that Dev was the culprit. Despite Jenny's antics, Winnie had never thought she would end up doing anything really extreme. Like Gabbar Singh, the most notorious villain in Bollywood cinematic history, Jenny was surprising everyone.

Winnie took a minute to catch her breath before pounding a fist against Reece's door. She heard the muffled sound of voices inside, and then Reece said, "Come in."

She opened the door. Mr. Reece sat behind his desk, his hair mussed and his tweed jacket removed and hanging behind his chair. He didn't look like the guy she normally sparred with on a regular basis. Raj was sitting in one of the two chairs facing the desk. He had his elbows propped on his spread knees and hung his head. When she walked in, he didn't even bother looking at her.

"Ms. Mehta. Close the door, please," Mr. Reece said. He had called her Winnie at the fund-raiser dance, but now he was back to calling her by her formal name. She obliged and slipped into the empty chair, moving as far away from Raj as she could.

"What's going on? Mr. Reece?"

"Congratulations on a successful fund-raiser for your film festival. However, there appears to be a problem. The fund-raiser proceeds were taken. You're not in trouble, but we need your help."

"Okay . . ."

"After the film festival I asked Jenny Dickens about the fund-raiser money. She stated that there had been a last-minute change, authorized by you, and she gave the cash box to Dev Khanna. I spoke to Dev this morning, and he claimed he didn't have it—"

"That's because he never took it," Winnie rushed in. She leaned forward against the desk. "I never authorized any-thing. Mr. Reece, he was with me the entire time."

Mr. Reece's voice was slow and soothing. "We completely understand that you believe Dev is innocent. I've known Dev for years, and he's always been an excellent student, but the funds were found in a plastic bag in his locker."

"What?"

Mr. Reece sighed and pinched the bridge of his nose. "I'm sorry, but it's school protocol to check the student's personal belongings if there is a concern about theft or activity that violates school policy, and when Dev opened his locker this morning, the bag was in plain sight."

"Dev's locker is broken. He's been trying to get the school to fix it forever. His whole hall knows about it. Facilities has multiple requests that he logged for repairs. Anyone could have put it there!"

She looked down at Raj, who was still sitting in the same position as when she had walked in. "Raj, you knew that Jenny was slated for the last shift, too."

Even though Raj's words were mumbled, each one hit her like an ice pick. "Jenny told me she gave the money to Dev, and I believe her. I was with her that night, and she didn't have it with her."

Winnie sank in her seat. "Are you seriously covering for her? How could you?"

"I told you he was bad news," Raj said, looking down at his hands.

"No, Jenny is bad news. She's threatened me before. You know that. You're just jealous because Dev—"

"I'm sorry, Winnie."

Holy baby Shah Rukh Khan.

Instead of screaming like she desperately wanted to,

she turned to Mr. Reece and said, "Dev's locker is broken. That scum-sucking, soulless demon from the bowels of hell must've gotten in and planted the evidence. She deserves to go down for theft, bullying, and being a stalker. I'm going to talk to the dean about it and lodge a complaint. You're such a rules guy, right, Mr. Reece? I bet you'd appreciate that."

"Winnie," Raj said with a sigh. "Leave Jenny alone."

Winnie pointed a finger at him and, in her best impression of Shatrughan Sinha, yelled, "Khamosh! Quiet. I can't believe you've forgotten so fast how terrible she was to you after you broke up with her."

"Okay, you two," Mr. Reece said. "Winnie, Dev has been excused for the day, but the suspension is probationary until we get to the bottom of this. Because we understand his locker was broken, we're not going to expel him yet."

"Not ever, Mr. Reece. He didn't do it!" Winnie's palms were white with red crescent nail marks from squeezing her fists so tight. She wasn't going to let Dev get expelled. No way was that happening when she knew Jenny and Raj were behind it.

"The reason I'm telling you this is because I've spoken with Dean Elgeway and he's promised that he'll let me lead the investigation quietly. Parents, of course, will have to be contacted. I'm asking you and Raj to be mature and handle this like adults. Unfortunately, because the evidence is clear at this point, Dev won't be able to show his feature at the film festival unless Jenny or a third party comes forward. If he's found innocent before the festival, then he can be readmitted to the lineup."

Winnie felt the burning in her throat of fresh tears. "Mr. Reece, he needs this film-festival credit for his creative portfolio. He's counting on this festival to feature his movie, especially with Gurinder Chadha being there. It's the chance of a lifetime for him. What if his name isn't cleared in time?"

Mr. Reece shook his head.

"It's a plant, Mr. Reece! You have to see that!" She slammed her hands down at the edge of his desk.

"Winnie, I'm sorry, but there is nothing I can do. That's my final word on the matter. I have to follow school rules even though I sympathize with your position."

He folded his fingers together and leaned forward on his desk. His voice sounded heavy with sadness. "If either of you interferes in the investigation, or if you ignore my rules about including Dev in the festival, you'll be stripped of your duties and film-club titles. There will also be a mandatory suspension."

"This is total—"

"Are. We. Clear?"

Winnie folded her arms across her chest. "Fine."

"So we aren't in trouble if we cooperate? We're excused?" Raj asked.

"For now, unless you *did* take part in all of this."

Raj shook his head.

"Winnie," Mr. Reece said. "Are you still willing to chair the festival despite Dev?"

Great, now she had to choose between her future and her new boyfriend, something that she hadn't seen coming.

"I'm still in, but I want to help nail Jenny's coffin shut. She's behind this."

Raj leaned forward and tried to touch her hand. "Winnie, I—"

"Don't," she said to Raj as she jerked away. "Just don't."

"Okay, enough," Mr. Reece interjected. "The film-club meeting has been canceled today. I asked Raj to email a notice to the members."

Winnie got up and stormed from Mr. Reece's office, banging the door with as much force as possible. She didn't care if it pissed him off. She had to find Dev and talk to him. She had to know what he was going to do and how they would get him out of this situation. This was all her fault. Dev wouldn't have been targeted if she'd dealt with Jenny sooner.

She jogged down the hallway and out through the main doors at the other end of the school. She had never cut a class in her entire time at Princeton Academy for the Arts and Sciences, but she was going to do it today. She ran toward her car, parked in the student parking lot, and hesitated when she spotted a familiar black sedan at the end of her row. Winnie slowed until she could read the license plate clearly, and then she sped up again. Dev got out of his car and strode toward her. When they were close, Winnie launched herself at him.

His arms encircled her and they held on to each other. Winnie felt her grip on her tears slipping. She sniffed as she buried her face in his neck and let out a shuddering breath. How could everything make sense one moment and be in complete chaos the next? She and Dev hadn't reached their happy ending after all.

19

DOSTANA / FRIENDSHIP
★★☆☆☆

I know this movie did great at the box offices overseas, but I don't like it. No matter what, lying is always a terrible move. Sorry, hunky hero. Put those pecs away. I want honesty first. You can't flex your way out of this one.

Winnie thought about the cultural significance of sharing food as she and Dev went out to grab lunch at an Indian restaurant. They stopped at the Dosa Hut in Princeton, where they ordered two large masala dosas. Winnie waited as the two-foot-long paper-thin crepe-like shell stuffed with spicy potato and onions was placed in front of her. She poked at the dosa shell until it cracked and then dug in, dipping occasionally into the sambar and coconut chutney.

After they had eaten in silence, Dev reached across the table and slipped his hand over Winnie's. "This is an interesting place," he said, looking around.

"The dosas are really good, though, right?"

He smiled, and Winnie saw the sadness in his face, even

though he was trying to do the whole nonchalant look that had fooled her so well for all those years.

"Dev," she said, her voice cracking.

"Are we going to talk about what happened today? Because I really don't want to talk about it. We've been good for the last hour or so."

"Dev . . . come on. I know we're, well, new and everything, but you know you can talk to me."

"I didn't do it, Winnie. You know I didn't do it."

"Of course I know you didn't take the money." She gripped his fingers with a bruising force. "Not only do I know that you would never do something like that, but you were also with me the entire night. I told Reece. Did you go to your locker in the morning?"

"No, I didn't need anything for first period. I was in homeroom when Reece called me. He asked me what I did after the festival and wouldn't tell me what it was about. I told them exactly what happened and where I was the entire time. They asked me to open my locker. I knew there was nothing in there, but when it opened, the money was sitting there. It wasn't even hidden or anything. How stupid do they think I am?"

"Raj backed up Jenny's story. I backed up yours. It's now a he-said-she-said thing."

"Reece told me they were suspending me for two days and notifying my mother. He was totally condescending when he spoke to me. Like he was channeling Amitabh Bachchan in *Mohabbatein*. You know, powerful educator who treats the student as inferior."

Winnie smiled. "You made a Bollywood movie reference."

The corner of Dev's lip quirked. "I did. I danced for you, too."

"You did," Winnie said. She leaned forward and kissed Dev's cheek. She reached for the check, which had been discreetly left at the edge of their table.

"I got it," Dev said, and took it from her.

She was about to argue, but her phone started buzzing. When she saw that it was Raj, she moved to decline the call.

"Go ahead. We're almost done. I can meet you outside."

Winnie sighed. "Okay, I'll be like two seconds." She got up and wove through the cluttered tables and chairs toward the exit.

"Kamina, kutta, sala," she said sweetly when she answered.

"Listen, I may be a bastard right now, but I'm not going to help that asshole, especially with the information I just found out."

Winnie peered through the glass at her boyfriend. Dev was handing a few bills over to the waitress. "You have five seconds before I hang up on you."

"No matter what you think, I still want to help you. We were friends before we dated."

"Raj, spit it out."

"Dev's name. It's shortened. He's registered with the school as Dev Khanna, but my mom's friend's cousin is good friends with his mom, and his real name is Ramdev. His name starts with an *R*. He knows about your prophecy and he lied to you. I don't get why he didn't tell you sooner."

She looked at Dev through the restaurant window as he finished paying. *No way.*

"Raj, Dev is not a liar. You are."

"Oh yeah? Ask him. He's been going by Dev for everything. Class rosters, online presence, whatever. But his birth name is different. Don't you think if he can lie about this, he can lie about stealing the film-club money?"

The dosa she'd enjoyed turned in her stomach, weighing down on her. "No, *you're* lying. Dev wouldn't do this to me."

"Why would I lie to you about this? Listen, I know you hate me, but like I said, we were together for a long time. I'm the one who, despite everything, knows you better than anyone. And you know me."

Winnie didn't want to hear any more. She couldn't hear any more. She ended the call when Dev stepped outside.

"Everything okay?" he said.

"Let me see your driver's license."

He hesitated. "You want to see my license?"

"Yes," she said, and waited.

"Winnie."

"Now, Dev."

He pulled out his wallet and paused a moment before

he passed her his license. She snatched it from him and searched for his name. There it was, in plain sight: RAMDEV KUMAR KHANNA.

"I was going to tell you. I tried to, but . . ."

She tossed the license against his chest. "Why didn't you? Why did you lie to me about this one thing that I shared with you that you knew was such a big deal for me?"

"I didn't exactly lie. . . ."

"A lie by omission is still a lie, Dev! Why did you do it?"

"You know I've wanted to be with you since freshman year."

"Is it because I used to be Raj's girlfriend and now you want to get back at him?"

"No! Winnie, it's important to me that you like me for who I am. Not like with Raj—"

"What about Raj?"

"Well, we all know you only dated him for your star chart, not because you really liked him. That's pretty easy to see."

Her mouth fell open. "Is that the type of person you think I am? Of course I liked him! What kind of human being does that make me if I stayed with the same guy for three years just because of an astrology prediction?"

"But you never loved him."

Guilt cast a shadow over her heart. "That's none of your business."

"Of course it's my business!" He took a step forward, and

Winnie retreated. He held his hands up as if to show her that he wasn't going to touch her.

"If you loved Raj, then I never would've had a chance now. You'd try to make things work with him. I wanted things to be different for you and me."

"You're not getting it, Dev. I thought I was making my own choices when you and I started seeing each other. I was creating the destiny that *I* wanted for myself. How do you think I feel now that I know I've been manipulated? You played me."

He stepped closer, cupping her face in her hands, and she felt his calloused thumbs brushing away her hot, angry tears. "I wanted you before I heard about the prophecy."

"But you *lied*," she said. "Now I can't be sure if I'm making this choice on my own or if . . . To think I almost gave up the co-chair spot because Reece doesn't want you in the festival anymore."

His hand dropped limp at his side. "What? You're still festival chair? After what Reece has done to me, I can't believe you're still a part of that."

"What, did you expect me to quit?"

"Yes, actually. Because your boyfriend got suspended."

The word *boyfriend* was like a kick to the gut. When she didn't say anything, Dev started toward his car. "Well, I guess I have answers, too. Don't you see, Winnie? This is why I didn't tell you my full name. I'm just a rebound to you."

"You were never a rebound," Winnie said, running the back of her hand over her nose. She couldn't stop crying now. "I'm trying to be smart, Dev. Unlike you, who decided lying was the best way to get what you wanted. Do you think I can try to help you clear your name if I'm out of the film festival altogether? Or are you looking for me to make some grand movie gesture?"

"Just as long as you get what you want, right? Look, I don't want to be another casualty in your attempt to prove destiny wrong. You obviously believe in fate, and that means that while you and I were together, you never believed in me. That's the only reason I could think of to explain how you'd easily pick your future over your future with me."

His words only made her cry harder. He got in his car before the next sob released from her chest.

"I've got to go," he said, and roared out of the parking lot. She didn't know how long she stood there. She snapped out of her haze when her phone started buzzing. She answered when she saw Bridget's name.

"Winnie? Dev called and said that he left you at Dosa Hut and for me to go pick you up. Are you okay? What happened?"

Winnie collapsed on the sidewalk. She told Bridget the story through sniffles.

"Are you kidding me? What are you thinking?"

Winnie felt as if Bridget had slapped her across the face with her angry retort. "What? Why would you say that?"

"Winnie, is NYU that important to you that you'll dick over someone who obviously is in love with you? Who you're supposed to be in love with?"

"I'm not—he's not—Dev doesn't love me. I don't love him." *I think.*

"Obviously not if screwing him over was so easy. Winnie, you should've walked out on Reece."

"I didn't walk out on Reece because I need to be in charge to help clear his name. How can I do that if I'm not chair?"

"And as a side benefit, you still get what you want out of the whole situation. Dev is facing expulsion because your ex-boyfriend's girl is an evil mastermind. Dev was right. You were never into him the way he was into you if it was that easy to choose college over your relationship. His name is a stupid excuse. If I'd known his name would make you crazy, I would've told you last week when I . . . Crap."

"No. No, no, no, no. Bridget, please tell me you didn't know."

There was a long pause. "Henry told me, and I told Dev that he had to say something."

"Henry, you, and Dev." Winnie squeezed her eyes shut and rocked. "How many other people know? I've been trying so hard to come to terms with this on my own, and you guys all lied to me. You didn't tell me about Raj dating Jenny, either, a few months ago."

"Are you seriously holding that against me?"

"It's twice in the same year. Raj at least told me the truth."

"Then maybe you guys really do deserve each other."

"For you to judge me when you're the one who's wrong is bullshit." She didn't care that the couple parking in front of the restaurant was staring at her.

"If that's what helps you sleep at night," Bridget said. "You have your stupid festival now, and when you realize how much of an idiot you're being, call me." She hung up, and the line went silent. Winnie looked down at the screen and sniffled. Through blurry eyes, she called her mother.

"Hall-oh?" her mother said cheerfully.

"Muma," Winnie croaked.

"Winnie? You know you're not supposed to call me in the middle of school. What happened? Is there an emergency?"

Winnie managed to ask her mother to pick her up at the Dosa Hut before hanging up. In the brisk chill of late fall, Winnie felt her heart break, and the real thing hurt so much more than she could've ever imagined.

20

AMAR AKBAR ANTHONY
★★★★★

Remember my blog entry about how characters get their ideas from friends or the gods? Well, there is an exception to that rule. If you don't have any friends left and the gods are leaving you hanging, you can ALWAYS count on family.

Winnie was grounded for all eternity. Cutting classes was apparently worse than breaking into someone's house and stealing a bunch of movies. She was pretty sure that the tongue lashing she received was bad enough to cause lesions. Not to mention the two days of detention.

Unfortunately, she couldn't get out of going to school, and while she tried to get through her misery, Bridget and Dev were nowhere to be found. Raj, on the other hand, was suddenly available at every turn and continued to try to corner her for a private talk.

By the end of the week Winnie looked so wrung out and sallow that her grandmother convinced her parents to let her stay home, in fear of her skin color changing. She spent the day in bed matching up actors with characters in her current life situation. By two a.m. she was so drunk on Starbucks bottled mochas and sleep deprivation that she knew she had to get answers on how to fix things.

Winnie put on Dev's hoodie, booted up her computer, and sat cross-legged on her bed while she made the video call.

Pandit Ohmi answered after two rings. He sat behind the same desk, with the same powdered mark on his forehead, wearing a similar polo shirt to the one he'd worn when she first spoke with him.

"Vaneeta Mehta. I was wondering when I'd hear from you again."

"Panditji, I have a question for you. How does it feel? To always be right?"

He raised an eyebrow. "Pretty terrible sometimes, unfortunately. What was I right about, Ms. Mehta? Ah, did you find your love?"

"Like you don't *know*."

"I don't."

She winced. "Sorry. That was rude."

He chuckled, and she could see his belly fat jiggle. "Sometimes frustration is good for the blood. Anger is just another emotion if maintained in healthy amounts. What are you so angry about, beta?"

"Dev. And Raj. I was mad about Raj because even though he fit the prophecy, I knew he wasn't the one. Now I'm mad about Dev, because after thinking I chose him on my own,

I apparently had no choice at all. So, as you can see, my life sucks."

Pandit Ohmi laughed again. "Beta, why don't you start from the beginning?"

She told him about when Dev interrupted her during the first film-club meeting and about everything up through her disastrous call with Bridget. By the end of it, she was exhausted, but felt a little bit better.

Pandit Ohmi put down the holy beads he had wrapped around one fist. "Winnie, do you know why so many people consult astrologers?"

"False hope?"

"Hope is never false, beta. Astrology gives hope like gods give hope. Although your and your parents' star alignments speak clearly, that doesn't mean you don't have free will. You can do whatever you like, and your prediction may change based on your decisions. But if you approach it the other way around, if you make decisions to avoid your star chart, or to chase after it, then you're not following your heart, and free will has been taken away by your misuse of reason."

"I *did* follow my heart. But Bridget and Henry and Dev all lied to me, so now I don't know if I made the decision for me or if destiny intervened."

"So what if you chose the same path the stars have suggested for you? Trust your instincts, beta."

"My instincts," she mused. "Dev said that to me once before."

"He's a smart boy," Pandit Ohmi replied. "Have there been any other indications that Dev is the right soul mate for you? That you felt he was your soul mate without knowing he fit your prophecy?"

Winnie immediately thought about the bracelet Dev's mother had touched in the dress shop on Oak Tree Road. She also remembered Dev's unwavering support and love for movies.

"I wish things were more . . . clear."

"Ahh," he said, letting out another belly laugh. "So you *can* think of other moments with Dev that show you your fate. My girl, you remind me so much of your mother."

"What? My mother? Everyone tells me I'm exactly like Dad."

"No," he said. "Definitely your mother. Strong-willed. When we first spoke, it was because she wanted to ask me if I had manipulated your father into thinking that she was going to have a child. She told me that I wasn't a doctor and I needed to stop meddling."

"*No*. Seriously?"

He nodded and leaned closer to the screen. "She also was using reason to circumvent hope, but like you, she had to learn that if you follow your heart, things will happen the way they were always meant to. Look at you now!" He motioned to her. "The miracle baby."

"Miracle baby," she whispered. "That's what Mom calls me." She rubbed the heel of her hand against her aching heart. "I screwed it up, didn't I? I should've told Mr. Reece that I couldn't be festival chair because it's wrong to still benefit from the situation. I need to support Dev one hundred percent, and I have to figure out a way to help clear his name without being in charge of the festival."

Pandit Ohmi leaned back in his chair, and the hinges screeched in protest. He linked his fingers and rested them against his gut. "You can still make things right. There is always a way to change the future."

"Yeah—quit. There goes my NYU application."

"How does that feel?"

Winnie paused. "You know? Not as terrible as I thought it would. I've been stressing about it for the whole school year up until now, but choosing Dev over the festival feels . . . right. Thank God I haven't submitted my application yet."

"Does your future rely so heavily on running this one festival?"

"It's a guarantee that I'll get in."

"Beta, *nothing* is a guarantee. Trust me. I'm an astrologer."

Winnie sighed. "Well, the good news is if I leave the festival, I don't have to worry about dealing with Raj anymore. Or Mr. Reece. He is such a rule follower."

"And you aren't?"

"I think it's important to appreciate rules, but to not

follow them blindly. I've been going to film festivals with my dad since I was a kid, and he always says the same thing when it comes to movies. Bollywood should appreciate certain rules established by the industry like love triangles and musical numbers, but not every producer has to follow those rules all the time. Mr. Reece is the kind of guy who will always be a follower. He'll go by the book on this one."

"Would you do things differently if you didn't have to follow Mr. Reece's book? For the festival."

"Oh, totally. But I need the school to approve everything."

"Why do you need the school?"

"Because it's a lot of money to come up with on my own. I doubt anyone would come to a festival that I hosted by myself, either. The school has a built-in audience. It has credibility."

He shrugged. "You never know until you try. Anyway, I must go, but I wish you the best of luck, Vaneeta Mehta. Follow your heart. Oh, and those dreams you've been having? Maybe they can lead you to help with your problem."

Before she could ask how he knew about her dreams, he'd shut down the monitor with a wave. Winnie pulled down the screen of her laptop and collapsed against her pillows.

"Pandit Ohmi strikes again," she said. Well, he'd made her feel better about her situation, which she guessed was a good thing.

Since she didn't think she was getting any more sleep, she walked over to her DVD library and looked for some of her favorites. She had other things she could do, like write a new blog post or finish up her paper for advanced European film studies, but she didn't think she was going to be productive.

Winnie ran a finger along the thin spines until she found *Baazigar.* She pulled it off the shelf and examined the image of Shah Rukh Khan. She thought about the premise of the movie and remembered one of the most famous lines that came out of the film:

Sometimes you need to lose something to win something. Someone who wins something by losing is called a gambler.

"Film festival . . . ," she said out loud. "Pandit Ohmi said . . . holy baby Shah Rukh Khan."

Winnie dropped the movie as the idea formed in her brain. It was three in the morning. She couldn't wake up her mom and dad to ask them for help. They'd kill her. Who else was there?

"Of course," Winnie said, and grinned.

She opened her bedroom door and peeked outside. The hallway was dark save for the one night-light. After tiptoeing past her parents' room, she reached the last door at the end of the hallway and pushed it open. Moonlight filtered through the curtains, and in the shadows she saw a lump in the middle of the bed. The sound of loud snoring filled the room.

"Nani?" she whispered. She nudged her grandmother in the side. "Hey, Nani?"

Her grandmother grunted, but didn't move.

Winnie repeated herself, louder this time.

"Haan," Nani said with an irritated growl.

"Nani, wake up. I need to talk to you," Winnie said.

"Winnie?" she said. "What's wrong?"

Winnie switched on the light.

Her grandmother's hair was pointing in all directions. Her hot pink paisley nightgown with white lace trim contrasted with the emerald-green blanket.

"What happened?"

"Nani, we need to talk. I spoke with Pandit Ohmi again, and I have a plan to fix everything."

Nani looked up at her, squinting. "Okay . . ."

"You have to help me," she said.

Her grandmother sat up slowly and absently ran a hand down Winnie's back. "You want to do this now?"

"I'm going to have to tell Mom and Dad eventually, but I need a team huddle before they wake up. It's important."

Nani nodded. She swayed for a moment, then yawned. "Beta, I'm not as young as I used to be. Why don't you put the chai on downstairs?" She opened her bedside table, took out a flask, and handed it to Winnie. "I'm not going to have chai in the middle of the night without my medicine. I won't get back to sleep."

Winnie looked down at the pink flask covered in red rose-buds. She shook her head and took it with her downstairs. One thing was certain: her plans were going to be a lot more interesting now that Nani was involved.

Winnie knew that Dev wouldn't be working the same shift as hers on Saturday. If she'd been in his position, she'd have avoided herself, too. She hoped she was wrong, but when she reached the movie theater that afternoon, Eric was running the ticket booth himself.

"Dev is sick," he said. "You willing to help after splicing the last reel?"

"Yeah, sure. It's great that you work with your own film so much."

He stepped into the lobby. "Listen, about that. Winnie, I was talking to the boys, and I think that I'm going to start going digital after all. I know that I hired you a few months ago, but I won't need someone to splice film anymore. You'll still have a job, though. Just in a different role. I'm so sorry—"

"No!" Winnie said, holding up her hands to stop him. "I mean, no, don't start apologizing. I'm happy I get to still work here. And going digital is *great*."

"Wait, you're not upset?"

"No, not at all! This is going to be good for you. Wait . . . you're going digital. Oh my God." She stepped forward and rested her palms against his shoulders. "Eric, please tell me you're going digital before next week."

"Uh, I ordered the projectors already. They should be here by then. Why?"

"There are moments in Bollywood movies where a

character realizes their mistake and tries to fix it, usually through a montage. I need your help for my montage. But first I have to talk to Henry. Is he here?"

Eric pointed toward the stairs leading to the projection room. She patted his shoulders and rushed off to find the one person who might be able to help her pull off her crazy plan.

When she entered the projection room, Henry was working on putting back together a platter tower that held the reels.

"Yo," she said from the door.

"I'll be out of your way soon," Henry said. His voice was so cold that it heated her temper in return.

"Hey! Why the hell are *you* mad? You call me a friend but then lie to me."

"Well, you hurt my friend *and* my girlfriend. Duh."

"So, what, I'm automatically the bad guy? You don't even know my side of the story!"

He stopped what he was doing and faced her. "Life isn't like one of your Bollywood movies, Winnie. You can't press the pause button on a remote here. You should've told Reece to screw himself. I thought you were smart enough not to believe in a stupid horoscope."

"I'm so *sick* of self-righteous jerks telling me what to believe in and what not to believe in, what to do with my life and what not to do. No one knows how important my janampatri reading is like I do. I grew up with it, not you. It's a part of my culture, not yours. And yeah, I have a tendency to compare everything to a movie. It makes me happy, and it's worked for me. So screw your stupid judgmental standards," she said as she walked over to the closest projector and kicked it. A booming sound echoed through the room, and the film on the screen flickered before normalizing.

When the rattling sound died, Winnie pressed a finger to one nostril, breathed in, and then pressed a finger to the other nostril and breathed. She then sucked in her stomach and pushed it out in a few quick short pants.

"What are you doing?" Henry said after a moment.

"My grandmother does it. It's supposed to help with stress," Winnie said, and then tried breathing through her nose again. When she felt like her head wasn't going to explode anymore, she stopped and opened her eyes. "There."

Henry raised an eyebrow. "Do you feel better?" he asked. He was standing in the same spot as before, with his arms crossed over his chest.

"Yeah, actually. Who would've thought all that weird stomach breathing worked? Anyway, listen. I didn't do anything to you, and for what it's worth, after a week I know that I screwed up with Dev. I screwed up with Bridget, too, but you guys should've told me, Henry. Not cool."

He blushed but nodded. "Yeah, okay. I should've said something."

"Good," she said. "Now I have to ask you a favor."

"A favor?"

"Yeah, I need you and Eric to help me. When I first started working here, Eric and Dev mentioned something about flash screenings. I haven't seen one since I've been here, but from what I understand, they sell out."

Henry grabbed the back of the chair he was sitting in, flipped it around, and straddled the seat. "Yeah, but mostly in the summer. Why are you asking . . . *oh.* Winnie, this is a holy baby Shah Rukh Khan moment!"

Winnie laughed. "Exactly. In a Bollywood movie, the hero has to do something big to show the heroine that he's fighting for her, right? This is gender-role reversal. I'm fighting for my hero."

Henry's lips parted in an O, and then he grinned. His whole face lit up. "I'm in. What do you need?"

21

SATTE PE SATTA / SEVEN ON SEVEN
★★★★☆

Whether the movie is the Hollywood original or the Bollywood remake,
the message is the same: go big or go home.

Winnie sat in Mr. Reece's office, in the same chair that she
always seemed to occupy when there was bad news afoot.

"Are you sure this is your final decision?" Mr. Reece said.

"Yes. I'm positive."

"Winnie, I don't understand. I'm glad you're still part
of film club, but leading the film festival has been something you've worked toward for months. You spent a lot of
time begging me to bend the rules. Is it that easy for you to
give up?"

"No, it's definitely not easy," she said with a snort. "But I
think you're wrong about all of this, and I can't stand by my
beliefs and still be in charge of your festival. So I'm out. But
I'm not giving up altogether. That's the second part of what I
wanted to tell you. I'm going to host my own festival."

She had the pleasure of watching his mouth drop. "I'm sorry. I swear I thought you said that you were going to host your own film festival."

"Yup," she said. The idea had become more of a reality after she'd told both Eric and Henry her preliminary plans. She had a place, a crew, and a week to pull it together. "I have pretty much everything set up, but I am missing one crucial part. That's where I'm hoping I can ask your help."

Mr. Reece took off his glasses. "Why do I feel I'm not going to like this?"

"Well, that really depends on you. The student film festival is only able to accommodate twelve shorts. We haven't informed the applicants who didn't make it yet. Instead of giving them some bad news, I was hoping, with your support, that I could offer the strongest contenders a spot in my festival. Before you ask, this doesn't break any rules. I checked."

He frowned, his eyes narrowing on hers. "You want to use school submissions for your own personal use?"

"With the permission of the filmmaker," she said.

He paused. "Why? Why host your own when you could stay and be a part of the most prestigious student-run festival on the East Coast?"

"You know, I've been trying to think of a movie that could explain exactly why I'm doing my own thing, exactly why I feel the way I do about this, but I can't. Not a single movie comes to mind. This is, I don't know, *right*. And you're the one who suggested that I do something different, that I act like a leader."

He pressed his fingertips to his eyes. "I didn't mean you should start your own film festival, Winnie. Do you know how much time and energy that's going to take?"

She laughed. She couldn't help it. "I know *exactly* how much time and energy it takes, Mr. Reece. I've been doing this way longer than you've been film-club faculty advisor."

"Good point."

"So?" she said after a moment.

He adjusted the sleeve of his tweed jacket. "Where are you having your festival?"

"The Rose."

"A good location, I suppose." He looked at his wristwatch. "We can continue this conversation after the club meeting."

She shook her head. "I'm not going. I'll talk to Raj later today—I've put that off too long—but I can't see him now. And if Jenny is in there, I'm going to go *Kill Bill* on her ass, so I don't think it's safe."

"Okay," he said. "Fair enough. Thanks for letting me know about your decision."

"Sure thing," she said. She got up to leave, but he called her name.

"Winnie? As long as you ask for permission from the filmmakers and they give it to you, in writing, then I see no problem."

Winnie whooped. "Thank you, thank you, thank you! You won't regret it."

"Don't forget to send me an invite," he said as she yanked open his office door.

"You bet! And, Mr. Reece? I know you're a Trekkie, but *Star Wars* is way better. Maybe you should look into being a double for one of those guys instead."

She heard him laughing as she raced down the hall.

One confrontation down for the day, and one more to go.

Winnie spent a few hours packing up some things in her room, and then headed out with a box and a silver bracelet. She needed the time to get herself in the zone before she talked to Raj. She'd figured he'd be at the film-club meeting anyway, but according to a text from Jessica, he was absent, along with Dev, Jenny Dickens, and Bridget.

She got in her car and, for the first time in a while, didn't turn on theme music. The storm that was brewing darkened the sky and made the familiar drive to Raj's house feel ominous.

Throughout most of their childhood, Raj had lived in a small town house, but last year, when his father became uber-rich, they'd upgraded to a mini-mansion in Princeton Junction.

Instead of going through the garage like she used to when

they dated, Winnie walked up the stone path and stood in front of the large French doors surrounded by stained glass. She blocked one nostril, breathed in, then pressed a finger to the other nostril and breathed out before she rang the doorbell.

The sound of shuffling came through the front door until finally it swung open. Raj's mom stood inside the foyer, her hair in a low bun and her small belly stretching the thin fabric of her tunic top.

"Winnie?"

"Hi, Chaya Auntie," she said slowly. "I'm so sorry to bother you, but I was wondering if Raj was around. I have some things that I want to give him," she said, motioning to her box.

Chaya Auntie's surprised expression changed to one of irritation. "Did he know you were coming?"

Winnie shook her head. Raj's mother sighed and stepped back so she could come into the house. The door closed behind her with a resounding slam.

"How are your parents doing?"

Winnie bit back her groan. Stupid Indian small talk always made things a lot more complicated. What Chaya Auntie really meant to say was *I don't care about your backstabbing mother who didn't invite me to her pooja. I had one of my own.*

"They're good. How are you and Uncle doing?" *I couldn't care less and I don't want to talk to you at all. I really want to give this to Raj and leave.*

"We're good. You know, so busy with Uncle's work these days, but doing well." *We're so rich now and have so many better friends that I don't need your mother or your father anymore anyway. We're better off, so have as many poojas as you want.*

"That's great! Well, I'm glad." *You suck.* "Is Raj in the garage?"

"He's outside right now. Near the stone wall in the yard. Here, let me show you."

Winnie followed Chaya Auntie through the house to the patio doors. Thunder rumbled, but she ignored it as she stepped through the opening and onto the deck. Less than a hundred yards away, Raj sat on the short stone wall that separated his property from the neighboring field.

"Hey," she said as she approached him.

Raj whipped around. "What are you doing here?"

She settled the box between them and shifted to get comfortable. "I have a few things I wanted to return to you."

He was wearing a sweater that she'd bought him with the money she'd earned from her first paid movie review. He combed his hair the same way she'd told him to junior year, when he was getting a bit shaggy. It was the first time she'd *looked* at him in so long.

"Winnie, I didn't mean to hurt you when I told you about Dev."

"You were the only one who told me the truth. So thanks. Really."

"But after you guys broke up . . . you didn't come find me."

She swung her legs, the heels of her feet hitting the worn stone of the wall she sat on. A brisk wind whistled around them. "No. I'm sorry, but I still believe that our story is over. What we had—"

"What we had was real, Winnie," Raj said. He looked at her through bitter eyes. "You keep telling me that it's your horoscope to believe in. Well, it's my feelings. Don't tell me that I didn't really love you. Because I did."

She squeezed his arm. "I know. You did. And I loved you, too. It was hypocritical of me to tell you what to feel or not to feel. But you have to admit, Raj, what we had was Vaseline on the lens."

"Vaseline?"

"You know. Vaseline. Or panty hose. It's that old cinematography trick that makes everything dreamy and hazy because it's shot through this crude screen. Totally obsolete as a method now, but I feel like that's what we had growing up. Vaseline on the camera lens."

He nodded. "We were perfect together because we were given the perfect shot."

"Exactly. We were destined to work. And then when we grew up and started to figure out how cameras function, how *life* works, and what we really wanted—"

"Then we saw the Vaseline for what it was. A device. Your horoscope was a device. Okay, as allegories go, it's a good one."

She nodded. The wind was picking up, and her skin prickled with goose bumps. "I was so angry when we first broke up because of how you did it, because of the way you treated our relationship. I was furious."

"I know," he said with a laugh. "You broke into my house and stole your stuff back."

Winnie grinned, pushing the flyaway strand of hair from her eyes. "It's true. But I think I was really mad because you weren't the one. And I knew it for a while and refused to accept it. That we loved each other but as friends, not as something more."

"Like you want with Dev."

"Right. Be honest with me: Did you really want me back, or was it something else?"

He looked at her, studying her face, and then shook his head. "I'd never really *failed* at anything. And truthfully, I may have asked you out after Dev mentioned he liked you all those years ago, but that was because I knew that if you two hit it off, I'd lose my best friend."

"That would've never happened."

"Really? Because it happened this time after you guys started dating."

Winnie held out her hand, palm up. "Raj?"

"Yeah?"

"Mujhse dosti karoge?"

He laughed, tossing his head back and rocking with the motion when she asked him to be her friend. Winnie giggled as well, and for some odd reason she felt like she'd cut a string, something that was holding her back.

He gripped her palm and squeezed. "Only you can ask me to be your friend by quoting one of the worst movies ever made."

"What? That is a love-triangle masterpiece."

"Don't you think we did better?" he said with a wink.

Winnie smiled. "Yeah, probably."

"I never should've doubted you. You are going to make a great movie critic one day, Winnie."

"And you are going to make a great engineer."

She let go of Raj and shifted so she could open the box. "I have some stuff for you." The first thing she produced was a check in the amount of all the stuff she took. "Sorry for breaking in and taking all my stuff back," she said. "Izzat restored. My parents are all about the family honor stuff."

He took the check, looked at it, and then tore it in half. "It was your stuff anyway," he said.

She smiled. "You sure?"

"Yeah. What else is in there?"

She handed over a framed picture of them at a Shah Rukh Khan concert from sophomore year, a hoodie that had lost its smell and comfort years ago, a watch, and then, finally, a jewelry box. Inside was the silver bracelet.

"This is for someone meant to be your jeevansathi. Your soul mate. Thanks for letting me borrow it."

He sighed but took the bracelet. "Maybe I can sell it on eBay or something. Do you know how expensive this was?"

As if the storm was waiting for Raj to say the magic word, the skies opened up and started showering on their moment.

"Really?" Winnie said, slicking her hair back. "We were having a positive moment," she yelled. "Everyone knows it only rains when it's a sad scene."

"So not true," Raj said, putting everything back in the box. He hopped off the wall and reached for her to help her down. "Remember *Namak Halaal*? Amitabh Bachchan was practically having sex in the rain with Smita Patil. The first *Dhoom* movie and *Jab We Met* also had awesome rain scenes."

"Let's not forget—"

"*Dil To Pagal Hai,*" they said in unison.

Winnie grinned and squeezed Raj's hands. "Don't resent Dev. He doesn't deserve to be expelled because of you and me."

Raj hung his head. "I know. I should've told Reece about Jenny's craziness before the dance."

"Yeah, and you should've stayed away from her."

"I was an idiot."

"But you're going to fix it now, right?" Winnie said as they walked arm in arm through the rain toward the house.

"Fine."

"Thanks."

"Did you know she'd never heard of Debbie Reynolds?"

Winnie gasped. "Please tell me you're joking."

"Not at all. Then I made her watch *Singin' in the Rain* and she thought it was boring. She thought someone like Adam Sandler could do what Gene Kelly accomplished with his comedic timing."

"Stop. You're causing palpitations," she said, even as a glow warmed her heart.

22

RANG DE BASANTI / COLOR IT SAFFRON
★★★★☆

Aamir Khan, get out of here. It takes longer than one musical number and thirty seconds to put together a big production. Elbow grease, Aamir. It takes elbow grease, sleepless nights, and Mom's cooking to really make things right.

Planning the Mehta "flash" film festival took every spare moment of the one week she allowed herself. She was able to get the permission of twelve of her favorite filmmakers who'd submitted to the student festival, and she slipped Dev's movie out of the school database as well since his name hadn't been cleared yet.

The Friday evening before the event, her family and friends joined in the chaos as they set up the Rose Theater. Folding tables bracketed the lobby and were covered with stacks of pamphlets she'd printed at the local copy store. Henry had helped her with the schedule and flyers about the filmmakers and their shorts, but those hadn't arrived yet.

Winnie's father was setting up chairs for the panelists on the stage in the two movie halls they were using for the event. The setup would be simple, and it would be easy to break down once they were done.

Thankfully, organizing the panelists had been easy, too. Half the filmmakers who had their movies selected agreed to come. The other panelists were Princeton University and Rutgers Film School professors invited by Mr. Reece. He'd been surprisingly supportive about tapping into his contacts. He even said that he was bringing a surprise guest of honor, but he wouldn't tell her who the guest would be.

"Place is coming together, Winnie," Henry said as he carried two microphones with dangling cords to the second movie hall.

"Thanks," she said as she helped him work the wires. "I never thought it would happen this fast. It takes forever to do the student film festival every year. I feel like we've been doing it wrong this whole time."

"Maybe it's because you don't have to follow so many rules."

Winnie laughed. "Amen to that."

"I wonder who from school is going to show up?"

"Me too."

She only really cared about two people. Winnie texted both Bridget and Dev to ask them to show up on Saturday night. Neither responded, even though the news of her departure from the school festival should've reached them by now. Just as she and Henry finished in the second movie hall, loud banging sounds filtered through from the lobby as Winnie's mother and grandmother arrived with large boxes.

"What are you guys doing? What are these things?" When she got closer to help, she could smell the Indian food. "No," she said. "Absolutely not. Mom!"

Her mother brushed her aside, and said, "People have to eat, no? We're putting this in Eric's fridge for tomorrow."

"Mom, the whole deal is that they buy the food *here* so the theater can make money. You can't bring food without checking with me!"

Her mom set the box down on the nearest concession-stand counter. Nani did the same with the box she carried, and when Winnie pulled the cardboard flaps back, she found at least a hundred samosas. The triangle-shaped fried pockets of potatoes and peas were still warm, which meant that her mother and Nani had spent most of the day making them. Large jars containing homemade mint and date chutneys were squeezed along the side. In the second box, a towering mound of fried dough balls soaked in syrup produced a smell that even had Winnie's mouth watering. Gulab jamun. The devil's dessert. So sinful and amazing that it shouldn't exist. She covered the box again and stepped back.

"Nope, no way. Thank you for all the work, but this isn't helpful to Eric's business. He's not only closed for the night to let us set up, but he's giving us the venue for free. We want to make sure that he'll make money through concessions."

Winnie's mom motioned to the boxes. "Don't worry—we

spoke to him. He wanted some extra food for the cocktail party after your festival. These are half of the batch we made."

The sound of running footsteps echoed until Henry, Jessica, and Jai burst into the lobby. Henry had the most crazed look in his eyes.

"I smell samosas," he said.

Winnie's mother beamed as she started pulling the food from boxes. "Are you hungry? We have extra. Winnie, go get plates from the car. I have napkins and spoons, too. Let's feed all these growing children."

Winnie was quickly shoved aside as everyone crowded over the boxes. With a sigh, she admitted defeat and left to get the plates and cutlery from the car.

Winnie stepped up to the curb in front of the theater, pressed the unlock button, and heard the familiar beep. She found her parents' sedan parked straight ahead on the same side of the street. She was a few feet away when she spotted the Beetle parked in front of it. A slender blonde got out from behind the wheel.

"Hi," she said when Winnie reached her side.

"Hi."

Her best friend looked sad. Bridget had her hair tied up in a high ponytail, and her face was void of any makeup. Behind her lime-green glasses, her eyes were puffy.

"I broke the BFFL code," she said.

"You did."

"Twice."

Winnie rolled her eyes. "Yup."

A car honked at another driver as it roared down Nassau Street.

"I was thinking of you, though," Bridget said when the sound faded.

"You should've told me, Bridget."

"I know. I've been keeping up with Henry. He told me he was helping you, and at first I was mad, but when he explained what was going on, well . . . I wanted to talk to you. Winnie, I'm *so* sorry I kept it from you, but it wasn't my secret. It was Dev's to tell. I figured if he didn't say something by your birthday, then I'd spill my guts."

Winnie dug her hands into the pockets of her jacket. "We are supposed to have each other's backs. How would you feel if I kept a secret about Henry? I feel like I can't trust you to talk to me about things after this."

"But you *can*!"

Winnie nodded. "I get that you were trying to help me, but I can screw things up and then fix them on my own."

"Yeah," she said. "Yeah, you can."

"Hey!"

Bridget propped her fists on her hips. "You're supposed to stand by Dev, Winnie. He made a mistake. So what? I make them, and you do, too."

"I do, but you can't interfere by keeping things to yourself because you think I'll screw things up. That's not fair to either of us."

"Fine, but—"

"Bridget. Please. Don't interfere."

"Okay. I'm sorry. Really. Even if it's the worst news ever, I'll tell you."

"Ditto. And in case Henry didn't tell you, I dropped out of the school festival. You were right, too. Dev is more important to me, more real to me, and I can help him without being festival chair with Raj. I don't want to be a festival chair if the lineup doesn't include Dev, anyway."

"I'm glad. You're still my BFFL?"

"I'll always be your best freaking friend for life," Winnie said with a laugh.

Bridget started crying, and as Winnie hugged her, the tightness in her chest eased.

"I missed you," she whispered.

"I missed you, too," Bridget whispered back.

They held each other, supporting one another like they had for years. When a truck drove by kicking up smoke, they pulled apart, coughing and laughing at the same time.

"So I heard you made this big long boring speech to Reece about your plan," Bridget said, wiping an eye. "I wish I was there to see it."

"It's okay," Winnie said, lifting the collar of her shirt to wipe her face. "It was sort of anticlimactic. No one slapped anyone. There wasn't any strange music. Pretty lame, actually. Best of all, Reece offered to help."

"Wow, that does sound anticlimactic. Glad I skipped the showing."

Winnie laughed. "Love you more than Shah Rukh Khan, Bridge."

"Love you more than Colin Firth. Did you drive your mom's car here? You're setting up for the new and improved Winnie festival, right?"

Winnie grinned and took the plastic bag of plates and cutlery from the backseat of her parents' car. "I am. And my parents and grandmother are actually here to help. Tomorrow we're going to start with a feature from a faculty member, and then Dev's movie."

"Dev's? Does he know?"

"Well, I'm hoping he'll show up to see it. He hasn't answered any of my texts yet. He'll be the second in the lineup, which is probably the best spot since the Princeton and Rutgers faculty will still be around."

Bridget rubbed her palms together. "This sounds awesome. Amazing. Okay, is there anything I can do?"

Winnie draped an arm around her best friend's shoulder and squeezed. "There is one thing you can do. As you know, my blog isn't exactly the most widely read news source in central Jersey. I got a huge bump at the fund-raiser dance, thanks to your help, but that wasn't enough."

Bridget snorted. "Yeah, that's putting it lightly. You need to get the word out faster?"

Winnie nodded. "And to more people. I want to make sure that we have a crowd for tomorrow and Sunday. I know we have students from school, and we have some adults showing up, but it's a flash festival, so there's not a lot of time to prepare. You think you can help with the marketing and fill the seats?"

"I'm on it," she said. "I first need the username and password for your blog."

"Why?"

"You want people to show up? You have to hashtag the right things. The right things are usually 'Ranveer Singh,' 'Aditya Chopra,' and 'shirtless.'"

"Ah, the finest of Bollywood actors. Is that going to be enough?"

"Eh. I'll add Katrina Kaif to the mix."

"What about people who don't like Bollywood?"

"We're in central Jersey. Do people like that exist?"

"Truth. But to be safe, I'll have Henry post something on the school's website, too."

"Good idea."

They walked together into the Rose.

23

KAPOOR AND SONS
★★★★★

Sometimes the hero doesn't get exactly what he or she wants, and ends up with something that has the potential of being better. I used to hate plot devices like this. Now? Not so much. Just because goals change doesn't mean I do, right? #RanveerSingh #AdityaChopra #KatrinaKaif

WINNIE: Hey, I know you're mad, but Raj is going to clear your name today. I dropped out of the festival, too. Also, you hurt me when you lied. If we're going to try to make this work, you can't lie. That's not cool.
WINNIE: That is if you want it to still work?
WINNIE: I hope you come tomorrow. Make sure you're there by 6:15PM if you can. I have a ticket waiting for you at the front table.
WINNIE: Miss you. I wish there was an emoji for that.
DEV: 😔

Winnie was in shock from the moment people first started walking in the door, and she had to work at containing her surprise. Bridget's social-media strategy had actually been effective. She saw a few familiar faces and a lot of new ones. They bought food from the concession stand, stood in front of the film posters to read the summaries, and checked the film-maker bios on the info table. The banner in the entrance read:

THE MEHTA WEEKEND FLASH FILM FESTIVAL
A Precursor to the Princeton Academy Student Film Festival
Celebrating Short Films in Princeton, New Jersey

"Here you go, beta," her father said as he handed her a cup of soda. He settled in next to her and surveyed the incoming crowd. "How is everything?"

She looked up at her father and smiled. "You look good in your suit, Daddy."

"Your mother thought so, too, when I was doing my MBA."

Winnie looped her arm through his. "I'm sure she thinks the same thing now." They scanned the crowd until they found her and Nani leading people into the first movie hall. Bridget was at the front door, checking in the filmmakers, and the AV guys were making sure that the movies were ready to go. Henry was going to play the shorts from the projection room and address schedule mishaps through the night. Eric, along with Winnie's father, was going to troubleshoot.

"Thank you, Daddy," Winnie said as she wrapped an arm around her father's waist. "Thanks for believing in me and doing this with me."

He patted her curled hair. "I take some of the blame for your love of movies, so I can shoulder some of the work as well. You've done good, beta."

Her smile wavered. "I know I've been . . . uh, difficult for a few months."

"No, just lost. You're okay now."

She squeezed his arm. "If you had a chance to do it all over again, would you have gone to America? Would you have tried to study film even though Dada and Dadi told you that you had to be in finance?"

He shook his head. "I would've done everything exactly the same," he said. "I knew that one day I was going to have a daughter who would do all this so much better than I ever could."

"How did you know?"

"I followed my heart."

Winnie stood on her toes and kissed his cheek. "Thanks, Daddy."

"And I listened to what Pandit Ohmi told me to do."

"Very funny," she said as her father snorted with laughter. She hugged him again, and they continued to watch the crowd. She still had some time before she gave the welcome speech and thanked the theater and volunteers. Mr. Reece was supposed to arrive soon with his surprise guest, and there were a few other details that were still left.

Like Dev. She hadn't heard anything from him since he'd texted her that emoji.

When she spotted Jai in his suit coming through the front door, she broke away from her father to meet him. He was carrying a giant box.

"Hey, gorgeous. Very nice suit."

He grinned. "Thank you. Now that I'm free again, maybe I'll catch me someone as hot as you here."

"What? Whatever happened to Tara? The Indian Barbie look-alike you were at the carnival with?"

"Oh, we broke things off. Sort of."

"Man, I'm sorry. You didn't mention anything over the last few days."

"Because it's a 'sort of,'" he said, smiling.

"Ah. Well, you're better off, right? Come on, let's take a peek." Winnie motioned for him to follow her with the box to Eric's office.

She opened the box and removed the first trophy from the bubble wrap. The plaque read FIRST PLACE—MEHTA FILM FESTIVAL and the date. The figurine was a star on top of a base that looked like a film reel.

"I can't believe I'm really doing this," she said. "I went from nothing to chair, then to nothing again, and now I'm part of a team that's hosting a festival."

"You mean you're *leading* a team," Jai said. "This is the key to your NYU application."

Winnie grinned. "Yeah. Yeah, you're so right. Things worked out after all."

The door burst open, and Bridget came to a stop right

before she would have slid into the desk. "You have to come and see this."

"What? What happened?"

Bridget dragged Winnie through the door and into the lobby. "Winnie, *look*." She pointed to a woman standing near the info table, talking to Winnie's father, Eric, and Mr. Reece. Her hair was styled in a bohemian-chic cut, and the musical bangles on her wrist moved with each boisterous laugh. Winnie could hear her British accent from across the room.

"Oh my God," Winnie said. "Is that who I think it is?"

Jai came up behind them and leaned his head in between Bridget's and Winnie's before whispering, "Who do you think it is? Because I have no clue what we're looking at."

"That's Gurinder Chadha," Bridget said reverently. "She's supposed to come for the student film festival, but she's here. *Today*."

"This is your chance to really make an impression on your idol," Bridget said. She gave her a little shove from the back. "Go get her!"

Winnie smiled her least-crazy smile when she approached the group. "Mr. Reece, Eric. Dad."

Her father squeezed her hand. "Winnie, meet Ms. Chadha."

Gurinder Chadha looked real, but in a surreal way, as if she had walked out of her TV and stood before her.

"My daughter is the one who organized the event," Winnie's father said proudly. "She took care of everything."

"It's an absolute honor to meet you," Winnie said. "I'm surprised, since we assumed you were attending the Princeton Academy Student Film Festival in a few weeks."

"I was in town. Your teacher called and said something exciting about a flash festival. Since it's all the rage, I decided to come."

"Well, we appreciate your time."

"My pleasure. Is your movie in the lineup, Winnie?"

"Unfortunately, no," she said.

"Winnie has been a leading member of the Princeton Academy film club for years," Mr. Reece said. "The previous faculty advisor, Ms. Jackson, raves about Winnie as well. She may not write, direct, or produce, but Winnie knows more about film than most theorists I know."

"You're applying to NYU?" Gurinder Chadha said.

"Yes, ma'am. South Asian film studies."

"Interesting. If you are applying, your qualifications must be very impressive."

Winnie had to squeeze her hands into fists at her side to prevent herself from waving them in the air like a lunatic. "Well, other than the film club and film festival at school, I've attended NYU's summer film camp, and I've had a few of my movie reviews published."

"Ms. Chadha, Winnie is being modest," Eric chimed in. "She's worked at this theater for months. She has a special gift that I know very few people possess these days. She can splice film."

"That's marvelous," Gurinder said. "I have never met someone younger than the age of forty who can splice film."

"Well," Winnie said, "I love holding film strips and piecing them together. I feel like I had a part in putting the movie on-screen."

Gurinder reached into her small clutch and removed a business card. She handed it over to Winnie. "Let's talk after the festival, but I want to give you this first in case I forget. I'm in the process of starting a new project, and I could use someone who knows how to handle thirty-five-millimeter film. There is also a bit of theory involved. Would that be of interest to you?"

Winnie looked at Eric, Mr. Reece, and her father's smiling face before responding. "I would be honored."

"And if you know of any students interested in producing . . ."

"You should check the second short in the lineup. Dev Khanna is going to be a star."

Gurinder made a note on her phone. "I'll pay close attention, then," she said.

"We can show you around," Mr. Reece said, motioning to Winnie's father. "We are the chaperones tonight, it seems."

"Great," Gurinder said. "Let's get going!"

Winnie thanked Gurinder one more time before she rejoined Bridget and Jai. "I can't believe she's here," Winnie whispered. "I spoke with Gurinder Chadha. She's my *hero*.

Have you guys seen *Viceroy's House*? *Bend It Like Beckham*? I need to get her autograph. My hands are so sweaty! I hope she didn't notice."

"The surprises aren't over yet," Bridget said. "It looks like you have one more person to talk to before we get started." She pointed over Winnie's shoulder.

Winnie turned to look. Raj stood to the side with his ticket in one hand, examining a film summary on an easel.

"Do you want me to kick him out?" Jai muttered.

"No," she said. "We're good. We're . . . friends. Hey, Raj!"

Raj looked up and waved to her. He hesitated when he saw Bridget tapping her fist against her palm next to Winnie.

"You guys, can you go do your thing? We're about to start."

Bridget grumbled, but she grabbed Henry's hand and pulled him away. Jai followed.

"I had to come," Raj said when he approached her. "Can we hug? Is it weird?"

"Well, now that you are asking if it's weird," she said with a laugh, and then squeezed him around the waist. "Gurinder Chadha is here. Did you do that?"

"I may have told Mr. Reece about her schedule. He did the rest."

"Thanks. That means a lot."

He rubbed the back of his neck. "It's the least I could do. I don't know if Mr. Reece said anything else to you, but after I came forward and said that I wasn't with Jenny the whole night of the fund-raiser, Jenny caved. I don't know the details, but she spoke with the school counselor and admitted to lying and putting the money in Dev's locker."

"So Reece is going to clear Dev to be a part of the school's film festival, too?"

"Most likely."

"That's awesome! Thank God. I know that probably meant you got detention, but I'm really glad you did it."

"Yeah." He looked down at the pamphlet. "And I'm grounded."

"Wow, like a regular American kid?"

He laughed. "Exactly like that. My parents had to look it up just to make sure they were doing it right."

"Well, if you're out and about, it can't be too bad. Are you staying?"

Raj nodded. "Is Dev cool with it, though?"

"I hope so." She led him toward the movie hall and gave him one last hug before she checked in with her team.

When Eric called her name as she stood in the empty lobby, she knew she'd run out of time. Unless he'd slipped through, Dev hadn't come. The truth was settling in fast now, like a roller-coaster drop.

"The show must go on," she said with a sigh.

24

A BREAK FROM NORMAL
MOVIE REVIEWS . . .

I know that I promised you all an awesome review this week, but I've been trying to fix things in my life, so I've been super busy. I will say this much: You know how I'm always talking about destiny and romance in Bollywood movies? Well, there is something that I forget to mention. If you try to avoid destiny, you'll end up only hurting yourself. But if you go with it, kind of like a surfer with a wave, maneuvering the board and trusting your instincts, destiny can take you on one amazing ride.

Winnie was so happy she'd memorized her speech. After running through the schedule and thanking everyone, she teared up at the applause. With one final bow, she left the movie hall, and she snuck into the projection room just as the first film began to play.

"What are you doing here?" Henry asked.

She sat in one of the two folding chairs set up in front of the projection window. "I can't be down there right now. Let me be annoyingly depressed for a minute. Do you mind if I take over for the first two clips? I need a moment. Mr. Reece is going to handle introducing the first panel, and then I'll pretend to be chipper after that."

Henry got up from his seat. "Fine, weirdo."

"Appreciate it, Henry."

He shoved his phone in his pocket and left. When the space was quiet, she kicked off her skyscraper heels. Waiting for Dev with so many witnesses around was humiliating. At least she wasn't standing in the middle of a baseball diamond like Drew Barrymore in *Never Been Kissed*. That would've been so much worse.

In the projection room, she could get herself together. It was just her, the hum of the machines, and the sound of the movies. She dropped her head and let her long hair drape over the chair. The movie began playing, and she closed her eyes, sinking deeper into the seat.

She heard the door creak open, but she didn't open her eyes. "I'm fine, Eric or Daddy or Bridget. Whoever it is. I got things under control. Just because I used to work with film and not digital doesn't mean I don't know what I'm doing."

"That's good to know."

Winnie's eyes popped open, and she jerked upright in her seat.

Dev held two Robert's Sweets cups. "Sorry I'm late," he said.

"You brought ice cream."

You brought ice cream? What kind of hello is that after an incredibly long time of sadness and depression? Haven't you learned anything?

Dev smirked as if he knew exactly what was going through

her head. He motioned to the extra chair next to her. "Can I sit down, or is this a private viewing?"

She smiled and waved him closer.

He handed her one of the cups before taking the spare seat.

He'd brought her Kit Kats and vanilla ice cream. Her favorite. They sat in silence, eating and watching the images play through the projection window.

Dev scooted his chair closer to hers until they were almost hip to hip. He placed his cup on the floor next to his feet, draped an arm along the back of her seat, and pressed a kiss against her temple.

"I'm sorry," he said, dropping another kiss on her shoulder. "I'm so sorry. I didn't want to screw up my one chance when you finally noticed me, and that's exactly what I did."

She rested her head in the crook of his shoulder and let him pull her closer. She felt good for the first time since they'd fought at Dosa Hut.

"I'm sorry, too," she said finally. "I should've taken a stand—"

"You did. This is . . . amazing, Winnie. And I know you were the reason Raj said something, too. Thank you."

Dev leaned forward and brushed his lips against hers.

Click.

"So why did you do this flash festival?"

"For you. Well, it's for your movie but also for me. I

wanted to make things right, but in my own way. You know that priest who gave my horoscope prediction? It was his suggestion."

Dev laughed. "Of course it was. Winnie, I love you."

"I love you, too, Ramdev Khanna." Their lips touched again just as the theater burst into applause.

For a second she thought everyone had heard her conversation with Dev. Her cheeks burned as she peered down into the audience and noticed that the first short had ended.

"Shit," she said, and passed her cup over to Dev. She moved to the control panel and selected the second movie, switching to the next clip as Mr. Reece made the announcement.

"You're next," Winnie said over her shoulder. "After this, you have to go down for the Q&A session."

"What would you have done if I hadn't shown up?"

"I would have told everyone that you weren't able to make it."

"Wow, then I had pretty perfect timing all around," Dev replied. "Did you watch my movie?"

"No, why?"

He motioned to the screen. "Because I made it for you."

The lights dimmed again, and she pressed Play. The theater darkened, and Winnie leaned forward to read the title screen.

KISMAT

DESTINY

The title frame faded, and the dedication came into focus. The words read: *For Vaneeta Mehta. Circumstance brought us together, people drove us apart, but destiny helped heal all wounds.*

"Dev," she whispered. "That's . . . beautiful."

He ran a hand down the length of her back. "You're not going to beat yourself up over whether or not we're together for the right reasons, right?"

"No," she said. "No, I'm going to follow my heart on this one. I still can't believe I didn't know your name."

"I wish I could change it. Seriously. *Ram*dev? It's so archaic, but it's my grandfather's name on my mother's side."

He handed her the ice cream cup. "Looks like you have a surprise on the bottom," he said.

She really wanted to watch his movie, but because he had that sparkle in his eyes, mixed in with a bit of uncertainty, she took the cup.

She started tapping the object at the bottom with a spoon and realized that it was cylindrical. Her heart pounded.

"Dev," she said, her voice shaky. She spooned up the silver bracelet, the same one that his mother had picked up at the store.

"Yeah," he said, looking down at it. "I should have planned that better. You know how some movies have, like, jewelry hidden in food? This was supposed to be like that, but I think you might have to, like, scrub it clean or something."

She gave a watery laugh. "It's so gross," she said. "You bought me the perfect bracelet."

He took the cup from her before lifting her to sit on his lap.

"This is perfect," she said.

"Even more perfect than your favorite cheesy romance scenes?"

She kissed him. "Way more perfect than that."

Winnie jerked up in Dev's lap when she heard someone on-screen say, "It's my destiny to be with a man who gives me a cowbell."

"Did I hear what I think I heard?"

"Yup." Dev grinned. "Your story has been an inspiration—ouch!"

Winnie pinched his arm before laughing so hard that the sound had to be smothered with vanilla-sweet kisses.

No matter how crazy her love life had become, fate had helped her find her Bollywood romance. She held Dev tight as she thanked the gods that her Bollywood hero had finally shown up, with his camera, his smart mouth, and ice cream in hand.

FOUR MONTHS LATER . . .

Winnie hadn't had a crazy dream in a long time, but she knew she was in one when she stepped under a blinding spotlight, the only light in a pitch-black room. Her footsteps echoed like she was in a warehouse.

"What the hell?" She was leather-clad, diamond-studded, and belly-baring. Her perfectly curled and highlighted hair billowed around her shoulders thanks to a fanlike breeze.

"It is I, señorita." Shah Rukh Khan's voice echoed in the dark. A second spotlight shone a few feet away, and she could see that the movie star carried a red rose. He was also wearing way too much leather.

"Thanks, Shah Rukh."

He walked purposefully toward her, his spotlight following every step of the way. "Congratulations on getting into NYU."

She'd received the letter that afternoon. She'd berated Dev into applying, too, and he'd also gotten an acceptance letter. Winnie couldn't have been happier. "My boyfriend and I also have summer internships on Gurinder Chadha's new film. It's local, so we're pretty good candidates to help her."

"You've finally gotten the happy ending you've always wanted. You've met your soul mate, and you're going to college. See? You didn't have to sacrifice one for the other."

"You're right. Dev is . . . amazing. Thanks. For all your help. You've guided a lot of my best decisions."

His signature laugh filled the space. "You're welcome. But there is still one thing left to do. Are you ready, señorita?"

"Uh, yeah. Sure."

A booming sound thundered around her, and blaring overhead lights flipped on. Dozens of people dressed in matching spandex unitards posed throughout the warehouse space. The scene looked absolutely ridiculous.

Shah Rukh Khan snapped his fingers, and a drumbeat began to thrum around them.

"Let's dance!"

ACKNOWLEDGMENTS

It took a small, diverse village to write this book, and each and every member of that village has my deepest and sincerest thanks. To Alison Magnotti-Nagel, Smita Kurrumchand, and Laura DeSilva Romero, my partners in crime and the best friends a girl can have. Thank you for keeping me sane all these years, for reading my horrible work and telling me it was good anyway. To my incredible MFA mentor, Cecilia Galante, for being my cheerleader throughout the entire writing process. Your positive energy was infectious, and I'll forever be grateful that I met you at Wilkes. Thanks to Susan Cartsonis, a baller woman in the film industry who provided input and honesty when I needed it the most. Susan, thank you for loving my story. To Gurinder Chadha for her insight, edits, and support. Punjabi mentor of my heart, I hope you like the changes I made. A special thanks to Blaze at Movies 14 in Wilkes-Barre, Pennsylvania, for showing me how to splice film and teaching me about projectors. Blaze, you're as cool as your name, and if I screwed up any of the explanation in this book, it's all on me. Thanks to my agent, Joy Tutela at David Black Literary, who has been my confidant, my advocate, my therapist, and, most important, my friend. Because I could never forget the woman who believed in me and my writing, to Phoebe Yeh. Thank you and the fantastic crew at Crown Books for Young Readers. Your hours of time, effort, and energy are humbling. Last but not least, to my writing community, including my Desi writers, the Sweet 16s, the Debut 17s, and the Electric 18s. You supported me when I was at my lowest, and losing hope. I made it to the finish line kicking and screaming, but I had you at my side the whole time. For that, you have my undying gratitude. I hope I've done the story justice and made you all proud.

WINNIE MEHTA'S BOLLYWOOD MOVIE REFERENCES IN ORDER OF APPEARANCE

Chapter 1

QUEEN (2013) ★★★★☆

Basically, heroine gets jilted and goes on her honeymoon by herself. She finds friends and adventure along the way. The reason why a movie with such a basic plotline deserves so many stars is because Kangana is HYSTERICAL. Like, belly laughs hysterical.

DIL TO PAGAL HAI (1997) / THE HEART IS CRAZY ★★★★★

Classic love triangle (or square?) involving a music producer, two dancers, and a sort of arranged marriage to a best friend. *DTPH* is a masterpiece from the late '90s.

Chapter 2

WHAT'S YOUR RAASHEE? (2009) /
WHAT'S YOUR HOROSCOPE? ★★☆☆☆

We all know Priyanka Chopra played the heroine in this

movie so she could promote her then boyfriend, who is a terrible actor.

BAAZIGAR (1993) / GAMBLER ★★★★☆

Shah Rukh Khan was stretching his acting muscles here. He wears a horrible Zorro outfit in one of the musical numbers, but the twist in this movie is KILLER.

KABHI KHUSHI KABHIE GHAM . . . (2001) / SOMETIMES HAPPINESS, SOMETIMES SADNESS . . . ★★★★☆

Anything with Amitabh Bachchan, Shah Rukh Khan, and Kajol should be an auto-watch. Also, Hrithik Roshan dancing. The only issue I have with the movie is that Bebo/Kareena Kapoor sucks at crying, so her character is super annoying.

Chapter 3

STUDENT OF THE YEAR (2012) ★★★★☆

Thus begin the industry careers of three blockbuster actors. They were all young at the time, which is why they were perfect for this movie, since it's like *High School Musical* except we get to see Sid Malhotra's abs.

Chapter 4

HUMPTY SHARMA KI DULHANIA (2014) / HUMPTY SHARMA'S BRIDE ★★★★☆

I'm skeptical about any attempts at remaking a Shah Rukh

Khan classic. However, Varun Dhawan deserved an award for this movie. His comedic timing was on point.

DEEWAAR (1975) / WALL ★★★★☆

Two brothers, one an underworld mob boss and the other a respectable police officer, find themselves in a twisted crime drama. There is betrayal, family sacrifice, and a kick-butt mom.

PROFESSOR (1962) ★★★★☆

Think *Mrs. Doubtfire.* Sort of. A son needs to pay for his mother's medical expenses, so he disguises himself as an old man to tutor two hot chicks . . . and falls for one of them. Creepy yet sweet, right?

Chapter 5

RAM LAKHAN (1989) ★★★★☆

In this movie, we have police officers, stolen inheritances, and underworld stuff with Madhuri Dixit dancing like the beast she is.

SHOLAY (1975) / EMBERS ★★★★★★★★★★★★★★★★★

Oh my God, don't even get me started on how awesome this movie is. I'm not even going to tell you about it. Don't be lame—just go watch it.

MOTHER INDIA (1957) ★★★☆☆

A classic Indian movie about the power and struggles of one woman. Invest in a lot of tissues.

Chapter 6

NAMASTEY LONDON (2007) ★★☆☆☆

Katrina Kaif needs some acting lessons, but what else is new? At least the soundtrack is decent.

NAMAK HALAAL (1982) / FAITHFUL ★★★★★

This movie has one of the sexiest rain dances in Bollywood cinematic history. Also, Amitabh Bachchan and Shashi Kapoor look like they have SO much fun together.

BEND IT LIKE BECKHAM (2002) ★★★★★

A soccer player who wants to break away from traditional British Punjabi culture. Tons of laughter and a hot coach.

BRIDE AND PREJUDICE (2004) ★★★★☆

Think *Pride and Prejudice,* except with amazing Indian family drama and dance scenes. I just can't give it five stars on principle. Colin Firth will always be the only Mr. Darcy that counts.

Chapter 7

DELHI-6 (2009) ★★☆☆☆

Section 6 in Delhi is dealing with racial tension between

Muslims and Hindus, but everyone gets together to defeat a rabid monkey that's loose in the streets. Also, the heroine wants to get on the TV show *Indian Idol,* but her parents want her married. I don't know, this is all sorts of confusing. A. R. Rahman did the score, which is why it deserves at least two stars.

Chapter 8

AAINA (1993) / MIRROR ★★★★☆

Juhi Chawla is supposed to be the ugly sister in this story, and she has to marry the hero because her sister ran away before the wedding. Jackie Shroff lucked out, though. Juhi was way hotter than her sister, even before her big makeover when she took off her glasses and started wearing saris.

JAB WE MET (2007) / WHEN WE MET ★★★★☆

Shahid Kapoor and Kareena Kapoor's greatest movie together . . . and the one that ended their personal relationship. Kareena found her funny bone and Shahid found his swagger in this movie.

OM SHANTI OM (2007) / PEACE ★★★★☆

Introducing Deepika Padukone in a double role. It's a remake of a Rishi Kapoor film from a few decades earlier but still an amazing story. Try not to think about the fact that the hero and heroine are twenty years apart in age.

Chapter 9

BOMBAY (1995) ★★★★☆

Bombay was originally a Tamil-language film, and because it was SO good, the producers dubbed it in Hindi. Talk about a beautiful love story that is sad at the same time.

MUJHSE DOSTI KAROGE! (2002) / WILL YOU BE MY FRIEND? ★★★☆☆

You've Got Mail with a mistaken-identity twist. A love triangle ensues and godly intervention is required to fix Rani Mukerji's dumb decisions.

Chapter 10

CHENNAI EXPRESS (2013) ★★★★☆

Sorry, Shah Rukh Khan. Deepika Padukone was the shining crown jewel of this movie, and all eyes were on her. Deepika plays the daughter of a mob boss. She is avoiding marriage by running away. Shah Rukh Khan just wants to dump his grandfather's ashes in a specific spot in the south. He gets caught in the crossfire in this hysterical dramedy.

DILWALE DULHANIA LE JAYENGE (1995) / THE BIG-HEARTED WILL TAKE AWAY THE BRIDE ★★★★★

Iconic Shah Rukh Khan and Kajol chemistry. One good girl goes on a trip before she succumbs to an arranged marriage. One wealthy brat meets good girl on the same trip, and a

love story that defies friendship, family, and culture ensues.
sigh

MAINE PYAR KIYA (1989) / I FELL IN LOVE ★★★★☆

Friends who fall in love. A man who must prove his feelings by giving up all of his wealth. A gang of hooligans. What more do you need?

Chapter 11
DANGAL (2016) / WRESTLING ★★★★★

Dangal is based on the true story of a female wrestler in India. Since Aamir Khan is in it and he produced the movie, it was destined to be a super hit.

Chapter 12
YAADEIN (2001) / MEMORIES ★★☆☆☆

The concept of *Yaadein* is an interesting one, but when you start having songs that include an army of Hrithik Roshans marching with guns for NO REASON, the movie becomes questionable.

Chapter 13
AISHA (2010) ★★★☆☆

Aisha is the Indian take on Jane Austen's *Emma*. Now you

all know that Bridget's favorite author is Austen, and her most favorite book of all time is *Pride and Prejudice,* but her SECOND fave of all time is *Emma.* So obviously, I had high standards. *Aisha* definitely passes muster for a solid remake of the classic novel.

Chapter 14

GOLIYON KI RAASLEELA: RAM-LEELA (2013) / A PLAY OF BULLETS: RAM-LEELA ★★★★★

Sanjay Leela Bhansali is known for his cinematography, not for his story lines, which is why *Ram-Leela* is just another take on *Romeo and Juliet.* Luckily, he cast Ranveer Singh as his hero. When Ranveer flexes his biceps, you can hear women sigh around the world.

HUM AAPKE HAIN KOUN . . . ! (1994) / WHO AM I TO YOU! ★★★★★

Madhuri Dixit is my god.

Chapter 15

HUM DIL DE CHUKE SANAM (1999) / I GAVE MY HEART AWAY, DARLING ★★★★☆

An arranged marriage goes horribly right in this movie. After you watch a love story unfold between the heroine and another guy. GASP. Intrigue.

FAN (2016) ★★★☆☆

Because Shah Rukh Khan movies always become blockbusters no matter how bad they are, we sometimes forget how great an actor he is. In *Fan,* he plays a double role, and although it's a super-arrogant concept, he sorta kills it.

GUPT (1997) / SECRET ★★★★☆

Stop it, Kajol. You're amazing. Also, Bobby Deol in leather is like a '90s fantasy.

Chapter 16

KUCH KUCH HOTA HAI (1998) / SOMETHING HAPPENS ★★★★☆

Love triangle between a player, the new girl, and the best friend. Although I'm not a huge fan of the fact that Shah Rukh Khan didn't start liking Kajol until she became ultra-feminine, their love story is so cute that I couldn't help but love this movie anyway. I mean, can you blame me? It has a train scene, a rain scene, group dances, and a WEDDING.

Chapter 17

MAIN HOON NA (2004) / I'M HERE FOR YOU ★★★★☆

As Farah Khan's directorial debut, *MHN* pokes fun at some tropes while sticking true to what really makes a good Bollywood movie: secret brother relationships, great dance scenes, and a mind-blowing soundtrack.

AE DIL HAI MUSHKIL (2016) / THIS LOVE IS COMPLICATED

★★★☆☆

Ever since Anushka Sharma got her lip job, she looks a little weird when she talks, but this movie is really all about Ranbir Kapoor. He's breaking boundaries, and although I, Winnie Mehta, am a Bollywood purist, I have to admit that he has a few good movies in his wheelhouse.

Chapter 18

KHAMOSHI (1996) / SILENCED ★★★☆☆

The heroine is seriously a damsel in distress in *Khamoshi*. She has to take care of her parents, who are both deaf, and a lot of other really bad things happen. Buy TONS of tissues for this one.

Chapter 19

DOSTANA (2008) / FRIENDSHIP ★★☆☆☆

Not really funny, mostly offensive, story of two Indian men who pretend to be a gay couple to room with a beautiful woman who owns a killer apartment. Then they compete for her while at the same time continuing their charade. UGH. I consider this a bit of a Bollywood fail. The song "Desi Girl" has become a cult classic, though.

MOHABBATEIN (2000) / LOVE STORIES ★★★★☆

This movie has FIVE different romance story lines in it. One of them involves Shah Rukh Khan and a ghost. For real. Even though the three main leads barely wear any clothes and Amitabh Bachchan's dialogues go on forever, this movie is amazeballs.

Chapter 20
AMAR AKBAR ANTHONY (1977) ★★★★★
Three brothers, separated at birth, find each other again without knowing that they're related. Tons of comedy, dancing, and drama.

Chapter 21
SATTE PE SATTA (1982) / SEVEN ON SEVEN ★★★★☆
It's a Bollywood remake of the Hollywood movie *Seven Brides for Seven Brothers*. Even though it lacks some originality, Amitabh Bachchan plays a double role and totally slays.

DHOOM (2004) / BANG ★★★☆☆
Okay, technically *Dhoom 2* is better than the first one, but John Abraham, y'all.

Chapter 22
RANG DE BASANTI (2006) / COLOR IT SAFFRON ★★★★☆
Aamir Khan somehow convinced me to watch a movie where

you know the ending is going to have you sobbing. An awe-some story about history and corruption in India today.

Chapter 23

KAPOOR AND SONS (2016) ★★★★★

Never been a fan of "realistic" Bollywood, but Fawad Khan and his adorably scruffy beard make anything worth watching.

MORE BOLLYWOOD MOVIES RANKED FOUR STARS AND HIGHER

Action Replayy (2010)

Andaz Apna Apna (1994)

Anjaana Anjani (2010)

Baahubali (2015)

Baahubali 2: The Conclusion (2017)

Band Baaja Baaraat (2010)

Bhool Bhulaiyaa (2007)

Bobby (1973)

Chalte Chalte (1976)

Chandni (1989)

Cheeni Kum (2007)

Cocktail (2012)

Darr (1993)

Devdas (2002)

Dil (1990)

Dil Bole Hadippa! (2009)

Dil Chahta Hai (2001)

Dil Dhadakne Do (2015)

The Dirty Picture (2010)

Duplicate (1998)

Guide (1965)

Jaane Tu . . . Ya Jaane Na (2008)

Jewel Thief (1967)

Jodhaa Akbar (2008)

Judwaa (1997)

Kaala Patthar (1979)

Kabhie Kabhie (1976)

Kaho Naa . . . Pyaar Hai (2000)

Kal Ho Naa Ho (2003)

Karun Arjun (1995)

Khal Nayak (1993)

Khoobsurat (2014)

Koyla (1997)

Lagaan (2001)

Lamhe (1991)

Lekin . . . (1991)

The Lunchbox (2013)

Luv Shuv Tey Chicken Khurana (2012)

Monsoon Wedding (2002)

Mr. India (1987)

Mughal-e-Azam (1960)

Nagina (1986)

Na Tum Jaano Na Hum (2002)

Pakeezah (1972)

Pardes (1997)

Piku (2015)

Qayamat Se Qayamat Tak (1988)

Raja (1995)

Raja Hindustani (1996)

Silsila (1981)

Singh Is Kinng (2008)

Taal (1999)

Tanu Weds Manu (2011)

Three Idiots (2009)

Two States (2014)

Umrao Jaan (1981)

Veer-Zara (2004)

Yeh Dillagi (1994)

Yeh Jawaani Hai Deewani (2013)

Zindagi Na Milegi Dobara (2011)

ABOUT THE AUTHOR

NISHA SHARMA grew up in northeast Pennsylvania immersed in Bollywood movies, '80s pop culture, and romance novels, so it is no surprise that her first young adult novel, *My So-Called Bollywood Life*, features all three.

The concept for the novel came to Nisha when she moved to New Jersey after law school, and a few years later, she completed *My So-Called Bollywood Life* as part of her MA thesis. Nisha was fortunate enough to receive feedback on film culture in the book from directors and producers such as Susan Cartsonis (Storefront Pictures) and Gurinder Chadha (Bend It Films).

Nisha credits her father for her multiple graduate degrees, and her mother for her love of Shah Rukh Khan and Jane Austen. She lives in New Jersey with her cat, Lizzie Bennett, and her dog, Nancey Drew. You can find her online at nisha-sharma.com or on Twitter and Instagram at @nishawrites.